Finally Doc .... of
the Palace. .... nd
Frenchy, the .... lid
not seem an .... to
the blazing ....

Ben leaned down in the buggy and shouted across at Doc. "I'm watching your boys, Doc." Then he brandished the rifle.

Doc seemed painfully surprised at Ben's presence. "You don't give up easy, do you, Ben?" called Doc.

"No," said Ben. "I'll outlive you yet. . . ."

W. R. Burnett

is the author of more than twenty novels, including *Little Caesar*. His screenplays include *High Sierra*, *The Great Escape*, and *The Asphalt Jungle*.

BITTER GROUND

W. R. Burnett

BALLANTINE BOOKS • NEW YORK

First published in hardcover by Alfred A. Knopf, Inc. in 1957.

Library of Congress Catalog Card Number: 57-10303

ISBN 0-345-34733-1

Manufactured in the United States of America

First Ballantine Books Edition: September 1987

I

The three men rode in through narrow East Canyon, then turned, at a sharp angle, toward the faraway cluster of long, low wooden buildings they could see, through a thin, mirage-like haze of blowing dust, stretching irregularly across the gently rolling floor of the tableland. Although it was early spring, the day—with the sun almost at high noon—was very hot and dry.

The horsemen were dwarfed to the size of ants by the immensity surrounding them: impossibly vast vistas of distance on all sides, negligently punctuated here and there by naked rocks as tall as houses, rocks that had been eroded into fantastically grotesque shapes by the wind, rain, and sun of countless millennia. Here and there rose giant cacti three times the height of a man on horseback, looking unhealthily swollen and as if they had been pumped up with gas, and showing not only murderous spikes, but the innocent white flowers of spring.

The three men were covered with whitish alkali dust, and their horses were badly lathered about the necks. The men were known as Doc, Pinto, and Frenchy, and this was their first venture into this odd, high corner of the west, although they had all been long familiar with most of the other corners, some of them equally odd, from Cheyenne to Fort Griffin, and from St. Louis to San Francisco.

Doc was about forty, a little, lean fellow, with a dark, weathered face, brown hair that curled at the ends, and slitted dark eyes. He was the only clean-shaven one of the three. In fact, Doc even looked neat covered with alkali dust. He had a neat soul. He spread neatness about him, as other men spread disorder. He was wearing tight black pants out over his boots; a pink shirt, with soft white collar and black string tie, and a neatly creased black Stetson. A short black plains coat was strapped to his saddle.

Pinto, in his late twenties, was an ordinary-looking cowhand type, in jean pants, checked cotton shirt, and sand-colored plains hat—ordinary-looking, that is, except for one thing: although his left eye was a bright blue, his right eye was a whitish-pink like that of a pinto pony. A partial albino, his hair was the color of tow and his normally pale, almost white, face was blistered to a violent red by the desert sun. He had a three-day beard, which looked like spun silver.

Frenchy, whose age could not be guessed, was a French-Canadian, possibly part Indian. He was short, squat, and inclined to fatness. His cheeks were rosy, his black eyes snapped with vitality and humor, and when he was not actually asleep he was generally talking or singing. He was dressed somewhat like Doc, except that his shirt was a bright red, and he had tied a yellow silk handkerchief about his black Stetson, in lieu of a hatband. He wore both mustache and imperial, à la Buffalo Bill. Strangers always remarked what a happy, good-natured fellow he was. Some of them were now dead strangers.

They were all heavily armed, each with two Colts strapped on, a rifle in each saddle-boot, and fighting-knives on lanyards around their necks.

Frenchy kept looking blandly about him, quietly humming a voyageur tune. Pinto rode with his hat tilted forward over his eyes as the glare of the sun was poison to him, and he seemed half-asleep, nodding with the walking motion of his weary horse. Doc's sharp eyes took in everything.

He raised his arm and pointed. "See? There's the construction shacks. God, must be hundreds of men working. Guess our information was right."

"Hope so," said Frenchy. "By God, we're running out of towns, Doc."

Doc shrugged. "Yeah," he said. "Law and order is sure ruining the West. It's all these lawyers and real-estate men and sheepherders and women coming in; good women, so called."

"Good, bad," said Frenchy, with a laugh. "I like women."

Pinto merely grunted and pulled his hat down farther against the sun. He was longing for the dusk and coolness of a saloon.

"How far out from the town you figure they are?" asked Frenchy, shading his eyes and looking off toward the big wooden buildings.

"I hear about fifteen miles," said Doc.

Pinto started in his saddle. "Fifteen miles!" he gasped. "You mean we still got fifteen miles to go? Hell, I thought them buildings was the town."

Doc swore to himself, then pointed off to the south. "Town's over there beyond that rise. If the spur was already in, we'd be too late," he said. "I hear she's starting to roar already and the spur won't reach there for five-six more months. No, we're getting in just right. We'll be all set up and going strong when the real rush starts."

"What do we do, Doc?" asked Pinto. It was a question that was asked Doc a dozen times a day, either by Pinto or Frenchy. They had surrendered their wills to him—and for a very good and human reason. Doc had no doubts. He always knew what to do.

"I got it all figured out," said Doc, chuckling. "Don't I always? If my information's right, that is. Sol Reed's here.

3

Must have a gambling joint. I knew Sol in Dodge. He'll remember me." Doc thought for a moment, then smiled with grim satisfaction. "Yeah; he'll remember me all right. I was dealing in Dodge, making a fortune. Sol was across the street, not doing so good. We had words. Sol is not a fighter; Sol is a promoter. So he hired a couple of bad Texas boys to hurrah me and run me up a tree. They were very well-known boys and Mayor Dog Kelley gave them a real nice funeral." Doc laughed to himself. "Yeah, Sol'll remember me."

Frenchy chuckled in sympathy, then he went on humming his voyageur tune.

But Pinto was interested in Doc's story and did not like his oblique manner of telling it. "So you got 'em both, eh, Doc?" he asked, eagerly.

"Yeah," said Doc, then he took out his makings, threw his leg over the pommel to ease himself, and rolled a cigarette.

Pinto waited. He kept on waiting. Doc never said another word about his famous fight with the two hired gunmen in Dodge.

They were close to the buildings now and were surprised and a little awed by the immensity of the project. Men swarmed everywhere, with picks, shovels, and sledges, urged on by sweating and cursing foremen. Looking toward the north, they could see the gleaming steel rails of the new Southern Pacific spur, stretching in diminishing perspective to the horizon.

Pinto was so overcome that he took off his hat and scratched his head. But the heat and the glare were so great without his hat that he put it back on hastily, cursing. "Well, I never," he said, looking at Doc. "You mean they can lay track that fast? Fifteen miles in five-six months?"

"So I hear," said Doc. "Maybe less."

"Sacré chien," said Frenchy, quietly, just to be in the middle of things and show interest; actually he didn't give a damn for the whole Southern Pacific system, or anything else for that matter, except women, liquor, and fun. Oh, what a happy day for him when he'd met Doc! All that he had to do was obey Doc, and Doc saw to it that he had the money to buy what he wanted. Of course, occasionally, there was trouble, bad trouble. But . . . when, in this dog of a life, was there not? The Mexican swinging the pick in front of his eyes had trouble, but did he also have fun? Frenchy began to sing in pidgin French.

Pinto and Doc, looking things over, ignored him.

Now a brazen crash startled them and sent waves of sound out into the silent tableland, as a pebble dropped into a river sends out its circle of ripples. Picks, shovels, and sledges were thrown aside and men fell over each other trying to be among the first to get into the mess shed.

"Them boys are hungry," said Pinto.

"Ever swing a sledge?" asked Doc.

"God forbid," said Pinto. "Nor did you, Doc."

"That's an understatement," said Doc, and Frenchy interrupted his singing to laugh. "The only manual labor I ever did in my life is shuffling the cards. Manual labor is for idiots."

"Vraiment," said Frenchy. "And I have been an idiot in my time, with callouses on my hands. But then . . . I was only sixteen. I was not so smart at sixteen. All that I had was a broad back."

Doc made no comment. He was watching a big fat Mexican in a red shirt and jeans. The Mexican had brought his own dinner pail and was now sitting down on a pile of railroad ties to eat.

"That Mex's from the town, more than likely," he said. "Let's go talk to him. The more we know before we hit San Ygnacio the better."

The Mexican turned and eyed them mistrustfully as they

5

rode up to him. He was an old-timer and these three men looked to him like trouble.

"Hi," said Doc.

The fat Mexican merely looked at him. They all dismounted. Pinto and Frenchy stayed with the horses. Smiling, friendly, Doc walked over to the Mexican and offered him a stogie.

"Smoke?"

The Mexican hesitated, but he couldn't for long resist the temptation of a nice after-lunch smoke. He was tired of cheap black Mexican cigarettes.

"*Gracias, señor,*" he said, taking the stogie gingerly, and bowing slightly. He felt uneasy. There was a look in Doc's slitted eyes that intimidated him, in spite of the fact that Doc seemed so friendly, so polite.

Doc sat down beside him on the railroad ties. "Go ahead. Eat," he said to the Mexican. "Don't let me interrupt you. I just want to ask you a few questions. I hope you don't mind."

"Oh, no, *señor,*" said the Mexican, touching his hat.

"You from San Ygnacio?"

"*Si.*"

"Lived there long?"

"Was born there, *señor*—when it was only a little Mexican village. That is forty years ago, *señor.*"

"Oh, a real old-timer," said Doc, pleasantly. "Must be a good solid man. Congratulations."

"*Gracias. Gracias,*" said the Mexican, overcome. Maybe this little man was not so bad after all. Maybe it was only that the sun was in his eyes.

"So you must know practically everything about San Ygnacio."

"*Si, señor.*"

"Does Mr. Sol Reed have a business establishment there?"

6

"*Si*. The biggest place in San Ygnacio. Bar, gambling room . . ."

Doc tilted his hat to one side with his forefinger and grinned rakishly. "And girls, I presume?"

The Mexican laughed, feeling more and more at ease. "Oh, *si, señor*. Very pretty girls—not all Mexican either. Some pretty blonde girls."

"Good, fine," said Doc. "You see, we've been on the trail for some time."

"Oh, sure, I understand. As for me, *señor,* I am married twenty-one years. Children. I work very hard. No money for girls or gambling. Sad, no?"

"Very sad," said Doc, who heard him out patiently, then reached into his pocket and brought out a silver dollar. "For you," he said, offering it to the Mexican. "A few drinks at least."

The Mexican was taken by surprise. He wanted the dollar, and he wanted to refuse it. Desire fought with pride. While he was hesitating, Doc slipped it into his shirt pocket. "Oh, *gracias, gracias,*" said the Mexican, putting down his food and taking off his hat. A very fine little man, indeed!

Doc stood up and began to dust himself with his riding gloves. "Seems I know the marshal here," he said, busy with his dusting. "Man named Johnston."

The Mexican looked at him blankly. "Oh, no, *señor*. Someone has told you wrong. It is Mr. Ben Gann. Many years now."

Doc struggled to control his face. Then he said: "Well, what do you think of that. I've been misinformed and I'm disappointed. I was hoping to have a drink with my old friend Johnston." He paused, as if hesitating, then smiled. "Well, I guess we'll be on our way. Thanks for all your trouble."

The Mexican stood up and bowed, then he looked off and

bowed to the other two men. "No," he said, "I thank *you*, *señor*. Thank you for the money."

Doc waved, then turned away.

The Mexican stood and watched the three men as they rode off in the direction of San Ygnacio. Now he noticed for the first time how heavily they were armed. *"Bandidos*, no?" he observed to himself. Then he sat down and got very busy with his eating. "But he was such a gentleman, the little one." He chewed lustily, then he glanced off at the three horsemen, who now were almost obscured by the thin, blowing dust. "Alfredo," he thought, *"bandidos* or no, eat, mind your business. Leave trouble to the Anglo-Saxons."

Doc, in high good-humor, stood up in his stirrups, turned, and waved at the Mexican, who jumped up and waved his hat in return. Now Doc sank back into his saddle and chuckled loudly. Both Pinto and Frenchy turned to study him.

"Lady Luck's with us," said Doc. "Sol Reed's got the biggest joint in the place, and there's a sixty-five-year-old city marshal, Ben Gann."

"Sixty-five-year-old," Frenchy began in amazement, then he burst out laughing and rolled in his saddle.

"Well, I never," said Pinto.

"I know old Ben," said Doc. "He was quite a man in his day. You'd think he'd hang 'em up by now. Glad he didn't. I'm tired of shooting marshals."

They all roared.

Doc waved a long arm. "There she is," he said. It was late afternoon. They had made very slow time because they had been forced to rest the exhausted horses at intervals. They'd also cooked their supper beside a big rock, just at the top of the rise beyond San Ygnacio, which they had been able to make out vaguely, scattered across the plain in the failing light.

But now it was right in front of them, with lights winking on here and there.

"What's all that working there?" asked Pinto.

A large group of workmen were just knocking off and starting home, carrying tools and dinner pails.

Doc reined in and addressed one of the men. "What's all that?" he asked, gesturing.

"We're leveling off the ground for the cattle pens and loading chutes," the workman explained. "Railroad's coming right in here. They're starting to build the station over there."

"Thanks," called Doc, then he joined the others. "What a town this is going to be," he said. "Cattle-shipping, everything. When the big rush really starts in a few months, we'll be in clover, boys; in clover."

Frenchy began to sing. Pinto felt like joining in because the sun was down now and there was no glaring light to torture his weak eyes.

They caught snatches of Frenchy's song:

> *"Mais oui . . . baybee . . .*
> *. . . mon coeur . . . bonheur . . .*
> *L'amour . . ."*

"Always *l'amour*," said Doc with a grunt. "Goddamned Frenchmen couldn't live without that word."

"Mais non, baybee," cried Frenchy, clowning. "Bot eet ees ver' axpanseeve."

"Cut the dialect," said Doc, irritably.

Frenchy shrugged and went on singing.

They were passing through the Mexican settlement now—Old Town, with its battered adobe church and its many little adobe houses. Candles burned in the depths of

9

the cantinas. They heard the sound of a guitar. A Mexican was singing a slow sad song in a high melancholy tenor.

Doc called to a passing Mexican boy, who stopped and stared in trepidation at the three strange, heavily armed Anglos.

"Where's the livery barn—the corral, son?" he asked.

"You cross the bridge, *señor*, then straight down Howard Street," the boy explained, "to San Juan, then you turn to the right. It is very big. Urbey's."

"Thank you, son," said Doc, tossing him a quarter.

The boy stared in startled surprise, then grabbed the coin in the air and ran off.

They came to the rickety wooden bridge which spanned a dry creek bed, crossed it, and found themselves on Howard Street, a dusty thoroughfare, about fifty feet wide, lined with massed adobe houses.

Pinto looked about him in irritation. "Ain't there nothing in this town but greasers?"

"This must be Mextown," said Doc. "We'll hit the white part up a piece."

They rode on knee to knee through the deep powdery dust of Howard Street. Lights were going on everywhere now. Some place a honky-tonk piano began to play.

"Boys starting early," Doc observed, mildly, looking about him. "Hardly had time for supper yet."

"There's San Juan Street," called Pinto, gesturing.

Doc looked at him in surprise. "How do you know?"

"Says so," said Pinto.

Doc grunted as he noticed the battered wooden sign-board. It surprised him. Sign-boards were damned scarce in the West. And as he was thinking about this, he noticed something up ahead that made him chuckle and bounce a little in his saddle.

"Look over there, boys," he said. "On the corner. See? Palace. Solomon Reed, proprietor. Nice-looking place."

They stared.

"Mais oui," cried Frenchy. "She ees ver' fine place. *Bon, bon."*

"Golly," said Pinto. "Big."

They turned to the right at the corner, with Doc still chuckling to himself and both Frenchy and Pinto looking back at the Palace Saloon and Gambling Hall, passed a couple of old, weather-stained one-story adobes with candles burning inside, and came finally to Urbey's Corral and Livery Barn, a big place, which took in nearly half a city block. There was a strong smell of horse-sweat, liniment, harness-leather and fresh hay. Lanterns burned everywhere; some of them stationary, some of them moving as if by themselves. Horses whinnied and stomped and the voices of hostlers could be heard, shouting at the animals.

"Business is good here," said Doc, as they rode up to the cavern-like entrance of the barn. "Maybe we can get a real dollar or two for these crowbaits."

As they swung to the ground, a Mexican hostler came out to see what they wanted, holding up a lantern.

"Yes, *señors*?"

"Want to sell these horses," said Doc. "Figure to stay awhile."

The hostler looked the lathered horses over in the flickering lantern light. As he hesitated, a tall man emerged from the cavern-like entrance, putting on a short plains coat. Paying no attention to Doc and his men, he started down San Juan toward Howard Street. The hostler called to him.

"Señor Stafford . . . please . . ."

The tall man turned and came back. He was lanky, and seemed to have hardly any hips at all. His face was lean and weathered-looking in the lantern light, and yet he was young, probably not yet thirty. He was wearing jeans, boots, and a dark-blue flannel shirt, besides the coat. His big hat, heavily sweated around the band, was turned up at

11

the sides and creased longways, Texas style. He was not wearing guns.

A momentary impression—something about the set of his lips, was it?—stirred a vague recollection in Doc's mind. He caught a quick glimpse of a lighted barroom—a poker game—had there been trouble? It seemed to Doc that there had. A picture over the bar: a naked woman on a red couch . . .

And then as suddenly as it had come, the recollection was gone, and Doc was looking at the tall, lean man blankly.

"Horses in pretty bad shape," Stafford was saying. "What they need most is cooling out—or you'll have sick horses."

"You want 'em?" asked Doc.

"Maybe."

"How much?"

"I just work here, you know," said Stafford.

"If you don't do the buying," said Doc, a little annoyed by the tall man's easy, assured manner, "why waste our time?"

"Give you a hundred and fifty dollars for the three of them if you got bills of sale," said Stafford, taking a match from his pocket and beginning to chew on it.

"*If* we got bills of sale," said Doc, his voice taking on a slight edge.

"Men ride in every day with no bills of sale," said Stafford, mildly. "We turn 'em away."

"Two hundred and fifty—and we got bills of sale," snapped Doc.

Stafford seemed unmoved by Doc's manner. "One seventy-five."

"Two hundred," said Doc, "and that's it. I'm not going to give 'em away. That chestnut gelding of mine is a real nice horse. I'll shoot 'em first."

"Sold," said Stafford; then he turned to the hostler. "Get the saddles off right away, call Manuel and cool these horses out good. No loafing. I'm going to get a bite to eat and I'll be back. I want 'em cooled out good. Savvy?"

"Yes, *señor*," said the Mexican.

"You fellows want to come in the office with me?" said Stafford.

They followed him into the office inside the big livery barn. A huge, fat old man was sitting behind a battered desk, smoking a cigar.

"This is Mr. Urbey," Stafford explained. Then he gave the old man a quick outline of the transaction.

"Good. Fine," said the old man, nodding. "Go ahead, Staff. Get your supper. I'll take care of it. Sit down, gentlemen."

Stafford went out without another word or glance. Doc looked after him resentfully. Then he turned to old Mr. Urbey—known as Pop to the town—who was fumbling with the smeared and tattered bills of sale.

"He been around long?"

Pop looked up foggily. "Who? Oh, Staff? About two months. Lucky day for me. Good man. Sober, smart. No trouble. Don't even wear a gun—never! Too many guns in this town."

He was interrupted by the hostlers who came in dragging the three saddles and the three rifles that had been in the boots.

"Pile 'em over there," said Doc, then he tossed the hostlers each a fifty-cent piece.

"Yes sir," Pop went on, ignoring Doc's arsenal, "too many guns. I says to Staff, I says, 'Staff, you better take to wearing a gun; at least when you go uptown at night. Bad drunks, all wearing guns. They'll tackle you. Bullies, all.' Know what he said? 'Mr. Urbey,' he says—he always calls me Mr. Urbey; very polite boy. 'Mr. Urbey,' he says, 'I seldom go uptown at night.' Yes sir. And he seldom does."

Pop talked on. Frenchy and Pinto rolled cigarettes and

13

ignored the proceedings. They always ignored the proceedings, left it to Doc.

"Where did he come from?" asked Doc, finally breaking into Pop's senile torrent of words.

"Don't know. Just come riding in on a big fine bay. Not a gun about him, and as he come in from the south must have been through some real rough country. Renegades in them hills, south. They hit a stage now and then. Mexes, breeds, and still some of the wild bunch about—though Ben's got them pretty well in hand. Least they don't come to San Ygnacio no more."

"Yeah," said Doc, who had stopped listening. The vague recollection of . . . something . . . bad trouble . . . what? nagged at him persistently, making him irritable.

"Yes sir," said Pop, going on innocently, "lot of rough strangers coming into town now—and it'll get worse when the spur's in. Old citizens wearing guns now that haven't wore 'em for years. A man just about has to. But not me. I'm too old. Don't see good. Though I'm only five-six years older than Ben Gann." Pop laughed and almost spilled the ink on his desk. "Ooops," he said. "Yes sir, but Ben's a tough, lean man. Ain't got a belly he has to see around." Pop laughed, shaking his three chins.

Doc was not amused.

Now the three men were walking down San Juan toward Howard Street, lugging their rifles and saddles. Old Pop had recommended the Long Horn Hotel to them. "Right across from the Palace—Sol Reed's place," he explained. "Pretty fair hotel if you can get in. If you can't, try Mextown. Always room for Anglos there, though you may git bit by bugs." Frenchy and Pinto kept glancing at Doc. Something was wrong with him and they felt uneasy, just as children feel uneasy when their father is silent and irritable.

"How about I take that saddle, Doc?" asked Pinto, trying to break the silence and get Doc in a better humor.

Doc handed him the saddle without a word. Frenchy glanced across the street as they reached the northeast corner of San Juan and Howard. "There's the place, Doc," he said. "Sol Reed's. Look at 'em going in already."

Doc grunted. "We got to find a barber shop, get ourselves a bath, dress up, if we're going out a-courting tonight."

Pinto and Frenchy roared. This sounded like the real Doc.

"Oh, we'll go a-courting all right," said Frenchy. *"Vraiment, vraiment."*

"I figure to be dealing faro at Sol's before midnight," said Doc. "If not, there will be considerable trouble in this town."

"Oh, yes, there'll be trouble," said Frenchy.

"But we court the man first," said Doc.

"Absolument!"

"Doc," said Pinto, "let me have that rifle."

Doc handed him the rifle in silence as they crossed Howard Street diagonally toward the Long Horn Hotel.

II

They all noticed that there was something wrong with the marshal, and they exchanged uneasy glances and ate in silence. From time to time Berta would jump up and hurry to the kitchen, and Homer Smith would follow her movements with his eyes, which were a deep brown in color and resembled those of a patient, kindly dog. Fat little Luis Aranjo, as usual, sat minding his own business, but missing nothing. Poor Homer! Gone on red-haired Berta—her so lively and quick, him so plodding and slow. Luis sighed. It was such an uneven match. Then he shrugged. But it was not really a match of any kind. Luis was almost certain that Berta had not the slightest idea how Homer felt about her. Homer, like himself, was practically accepted as a member of the Gann family. Old Man Gann—the marshal—and his two deputies!

"Eat, eat, Homer," snapped Ben Gann. "What's the matter with you tonight?"

"I'm eating, Mr. Gann. I'm eating," said Homer, slowly, almost plaintively. There was nearly always a plaintive note in his voice, Luis decided.

Berta brought in the apple pie and standing beside Ben began to cut it.

"That crust's a little too brown," said Ben.

Neither of his deputies had the courage to contradict him, though the pie looked wonderful to them.

"You think so, Ben?" said Berta, indulgently.

It was odd how she always called him Ben, thought Luis, this tough and dignified old man who looked more like her grandfather than her father.

Ben grumbled under his gray mustache, but made no further comment, and ate his piece of pie quickly, using his knife. Luis and Homer both used their knives, too. It was the correct way to eat pie. Didn't they have the example of the marshal?

"More coffee, Ben?" asked Berta.

Ben nodded, then he said: "Homer, you through?"

"Yes, Mr. Gann."

"Get uptown. She's roaring already, I'm sure."

"But I was going to dry the dishes for Miss Berta."

Ben merely snorted. Shrugging, Homer rose slowly and looked about for his rifle and his gun-belt. Ben showed violent irritation.

"You left them in the office," he shouted.

Homer jumped, then he directed a slavish smile in Berta's direction, turned, and went out.

"Must you yell at him, Ben?" asked Berta.

"He's so slow. He's so moony," said Ben. "He riles me."

Luis wiped his mouth with the back of his hand, then rose. "Wonderful dinner, Miss Berta," he said. "The pie . . . ah, what pie! I'm going now, Mr. Gann."

As he was buckling on his gun-belt, Ben asked: "Things pretty quiet in Mextown, Luis?"

Mextown was Luis's beat. He had the confidence of the Mexicans and he could speak their language, although he was only half Mexican himself, his mother having been a Scotch woman. "Pretty quiet," said Luis. "A little thing here and there. A man beats his wife. A few fights. No real

17

trouble except when the drunken Anglos come into Mextown—then, trouble."

"The outlanders, eh?" asked Ben, bitingly.

"Yes," said Luis. "The new people coming in. They don't know how to behave here yet."

"We'll teach 'em," said Ben.

"Yes sir," said Luis, then he smiled, gestured, and went out.

Berta poured herself a fresh cup of coffee and sat down beside her father. He looked forbidding, a little like a tired, fierce old eagle. She felt that he wanted to talk.

"Damned outlanders coming in, ruining the town," said Ben, as if to himself. "And it's going to get worse, much worse. Wait till the spur gets here. Not only plain outlanders, but the bad ones will be coming in as they did in Dodge and Abilene and all the boomtowns. The wolves—they gather."

Berta poured him some more coffee without a word. She had never heard him talk quite like this before. She felt worried, unsettled.

"Yes," said Ben, "they gather—for the kill. I'm just a kind of herd-rider. It's my job to keep the herd quiet—and then fight off the wolves when need be." He took a long drink of coffee. "I've seen it in town after town—and now *we're* going to get it. Doesn't matter much for me. I been around a long time. But—you, Berta. You got a future. This is your home. It's a damned shame."

Berta did not know what to say. No use to try to minimize. In his frame of mind it would only anger and irritate him and do no good at all. She said nothing.

Now he turned and looked at her. "How well do you know that Stafford fellow?" he demanded, abruptly.

Berta could feel herself flushing. She lowered her eyes. Actually there was no real reason for her to feel so uncomfortable, so guilty, under the probing look of her father's cold gray eyes. There was nothing—nothing at all.

"How well do I—?" she began slowly. "Well, I've talked to him quite a few times. The first time, when I took the three horses up for you and Homer. Then—I, well, I meet him on the street, you know. He's very polite."

"He's a damned outlander," cried Ben. "Rode in from no place. Even old Pop don't know who he is or where he came from."

"Well—he seems all right," said Berta, lowering her eyes.

"Homer saw you talking to him at the store," Ben went on. "He said you were laughing and talking pretty lively. You'll make yourself cheap carrying on that way with a man nobody knows."

Berta flushed with anger this time. "Do you think I'm cheap, Ben?" she demanded, rising and beginning to clear away the dishes.

"No," said Ben. "Damned silly question. But other people might. Not our people—the outlanders. All coming in in droves. They don't know you from Eve, nor me from Adam. And I wouldn't be running around town in them pants any longer. You're no kid any more. You're nineteen years old. You got a woman figure. Those pants are too tight in the back. I saw some fellows looking at you and laughing."

Berta's face was almost scarlet. "Well, I'm—I'm glad you told me that, Ben. I didn't realize—yes, I saw some men laughing at me, too, but I didn't know why. I'll put a dress on after this when I go uptown—except when I ride."

"Don't be going up to that corral any more. When you want a horse, tell Homer."

"But," Berta protested, "like when Mrs. Graham wanted me to ride out to Ferguson's with her. Nobody was around. I had to go get the horses and—"

"Homer will get the horses for you, after this," said Ben, firmly.

"But if there's nobody around—"

"Don't argue with me, Berta," said Ben, harshly, rising.

"Seems to me you're mighty damned anxious to get up to that corral."

Berta flushed again. What Ben said was true. She was anxious "to get up to that corral." She liked Staff, she really liked him, and she felt at ease with him. He was so quiet, polite, no monkey business about him, like some of the young fellows she could mention. Oh, Ben would get the guns out if he knew what one of them had said to her and he was no outlander either! And then that man that hugged her in the store when she was buying the calico the other day. A big man, a stranger. Just came up and hugged her and squeezed her and tried to slide his hand up—well—best not to think about that! Ben would be wild. Ben didn't seem to understand about these things at all. They just happened. It was hardly a killing matter.

But none of that sniggling, suggestive stuff about Staff. He would look at her calmly, mildly, chewing on a match and call her "Miss Berta." He had gray eyes with little gold flecks in them. He was far from handsome, too thin and lanky and awkwardly tall. But there was something about him. . . .

"All right, Ben," she said. "I'll do whatever you say."

Ben was buckling on his guns. She watched him as he strapped the holsters to his thighs, then tried a practice draw or two. He was unbelievably fast. In the snap of a finger, there he was with a gun in his hand. It was almost like magic.

"One thing," said Ben, grimly. "Nobody can outdraw me. Never been outdrawn yet, or I'd never lived to sixty-five."

Berta came to him and pecked him lightly on the cheek.

"Lock the door after me," he said, moving back away from her, as he always did when she kissed him, as if he'd been stung. "Keep it locked. Either Homer or me will drop back from time to time to see that everything's all right."

Berta laughed. "I wish you wouldn't worry about—"

But Ben cut in: "Times have changed, Berta. No telling what might happen now. Keep the door locked.

He turned and went out. Berta locked the door, then she carried the last of the dishes to the kitchen and began to wash them. She could not stop thinking about Staff, at the corral. "What's the matter with me?" she asked herself. "I've never been like this before."

Berta had just sat down with her sewing basket—it was a caution how Ben could get through socks!—when there was a tap at the door. Berta sat up and listened. Things had changed in San Ygnacio, really changed. Not so long ago she used to sit alone in the house at night with the front door wide open. The tap was repeated, then a cheerful bass voice called: "Berta, it's me."

"The judge," cried Berta, leaping up and almost spilling her sewing basket.

She ran to the door and opened it, smiling. Maybe the judge would sit with her and talk awhile, even if Ben wasn't there. Berta hated to be alone; not because of fear but because she was gregarious and friendly by nature.

Judge Howard stood in the doorway, smiling at her, with his hat off. He was a big, wide man in his middle fifties. His face was broad, his cheekbones high, his head almost devoid of hair. He was always neatly dressed, in a well-brushed Prince Albert and a brocaded vest with a heavy gold watch-chain across it. He was not fat, just big. One look at the judge and you had confidence in him.

"Come in, Judge, come in," said Berta. "Ben's gone already. But come in, anyway."

"Why, thank you, Berta, I will," said the judge.

He followed her into the little sitting-room with its deep-set windows, its pleasant lamp, and its air of comfort. As soon as Berta was seated the judge sat opposite her. Noticing the sewing basket, he said: "Go ahead, sew if you like."

"I'd better," said Berta. "I'm getting behind on my darning. Would you like to smoke?"

"I would if you don't mind," said the judge, bowing slightly in her direction.

"You know I don't mind," said Berta, laughing.

The judge took out a cigar, carefully removed the band, then snipped off the end with a gold cutter that hung on his watch-chain. Sighing with satisfaction, he lit up. Then he sat smoking and smiling at Berta, who had taken up her sewing.

"I've said it before and I'll say it again," said the judge. "I wish I was thirty years younger—or even twenty."

Berta laughed. The judge was very gallant, always making nice remarks like that. It pleased her. "Now you know I'd be a terrible nuisance, Judge," she said.

"Any woman worth her salt is a nuisance," said the judge. "Just as any man worth thinking about is a pain in the neck from time to time. For those who want nothing but peace, I'll say this: they'll get all the peace they want soon enough."

Berta laughed, wondering if Staff would ever really be "a pain in the neck." She couldn't imagine it.

"So the old boy's gone already," said the judge. "It's just as well."

"Oh?" said Berta, glancing up.

The judge laughed. "Well, to tell you the truth, I saw him leave. I came over for a talk with you. It's about time we had a little talk—behind the marshal's back, I mean."

Berta glanced up again and studied the judge's big face. "I don't understand, Judge."

"Well, I'll tell you, Berta," said the judge, "the town's growing so fast and everything's kind of becoming out moded, including the law. We need more men. Look at me. I'm the mayor and the only judge in town. I've got two clerks, such as they are. Ben's got two deputies. Town's over twelve hundred souls now. And God alone knows how many we'll have in a year's time. It will be a stampede."

Berta's face was serious now. The judge was not saying what he meant. He was trying to save everybody's feelings. Ben was getting too old for the job. That's what it was all about.

"I just thought you might help me a little with Ben," said the judge, noticing the serious look and showing some discomfort. "I was thinking . . . well, I've got to the place I need a deputy mayor. Ben would suit me fine. It would be a step up for him. And then we could look around and find us another marshal to take all this grief. We might import one—Ben knows everybody that's ever hit the frontier. The important guns, I mean. What do you think?"

"It would kill him," said Berta, quickly.

The judge feigned complete astonishment. "A promotion?"

"Judge," said Berta, "try to fool Ben, but don't try to fool me." The judge lowered his eyes uncomfortably. "Tonight he was practicing his draw, as if he was twenty-five years old," she went on. "He bragged there wasn't a man in the West could outdraw him."

"He's right," said the judge. "At least none has."

"So you see—?"

"Berta," said the judge, "he'll get himself killed, sure. The real guns are bound to start coming in soon. And you know Ben. He'll back up from no man."

"That's right," said Berta. "That's his life."

A heavy silence fell in the pleasantly lit room. The judge puffed quietly on his cigar. Somewhere, a noisy little clock with a hitch in the works ticked on, then sputtered, ticked, and sputtered. Berta sat thinking about her father. She admired him above all living men, admired and respected him. Her first memories were of him, as her mother had died when she was two. He was like a rock, solid, permanent. But lately she had begun to notice the signs of age. The gray hair didn't matter; it had been gray for many years. No, it wasn't that. It was mostly when he got up in

23

the morning and began to get ready for his breakfast. He shaved with great care, not as in the old days whipping through it and talking to her at the same time, and once in a while his hand shook. And then there was a sort of stiffness about his movements that was new; and some mornings he coughed, coughed, until she had to go to another part of the house to keep from remarking about it. Ben was an old man—or getting to be one—no doubt about it. His unswerving determination to carry out his duties as marshal of San Ygnacio kept him going. Ben sitting in an office chair? Impossible. But that wasn't the worst of it. Merely asking him to relinquish . . . She looked up. The judge was speaking.

"I see I've got to handle it another way," he was saying. "I'll appoint myself a couple of new clerks. Young men who know how to handle hardware. And then if Ben gets into trouble—" He broke off.

"Yes," said Berta. "That might be all right, as long as Ben doesn't suspect anything."

"Oh, I'm sure he won't," said the judge. "He knows I'm loaded down with work."

There was another long silence, punctuated by the erratic ticking of the little clock.

"Berta," said the judge, "I wish I had a daughter as smart and understanding as yourself. You may get Ben killed, but you'll never break his heart."

"I hope not, Judge," said Berta. "I hope not."

And as Berta was speaking, her father was walking leisurely up San Juan Street, toward Urbey's Corral and Livery Barn. A couple of Mexican hostlers noticed him passing the corral fence, took off their hats and bowed to him. An unusual Anglo, the marshal, always kind to the Mexicans. In other towns Mexicans were slammed over the heads with guns if they got a little drunk, and thrown into jail. Not in San Ygnacio. Unless they were wildly unruly either Luis Aranjo or the marshal himself took them home. The marshal liked the old people—the ones who had been around for years, and many of the Mexicans had been born there.

"Good evening, Marshal," said the Mexicans.

"Good evening, boys," said Ben, nodding. "Nice night."

"Si, si," said the Mexicans. "Very nice night, Marshal."

Ben turned in at the cavern-like entrance to the livery barn and went into the office. Pop Urbey was sitting behind his desk, drinking a glass of beer somebody had brought in for him.

"Hi, Ben," he said, wondering what the marshal was doing there. He was not the type of man who made social visits.

"Hi, Pop," said Ben. "Where's that helper of yours?"

"Staff? Went out to get his dinner. Came back. Cleaned up a little work. Left again. I was sitting out front at the time. Think I saw him go in the Antler Bar. Needed a drink, I guess. Been working hard. Why?"

"He's a newcomer. Like to keep my eyes on them. Thought I might talk to him. The real bad ones are coming in, or will be soon. He might be one of the first."

Pop Urbey laughed at him and finished his beer. "Ben," he said, "you got a mania about the newcomers. Maybe some bad ones. Maybe some two-bit roughs. The railroad fellows are helping to make the town wild. But not Staff. He's the quietest young fellow I've ever had around this place. Ask Miss Berta. I've seen her talking with him. And you know Miss Berta is not going around talking to roughs."

Ben merely compressed his lips at this. "Antler, you say? Thanks, Pop."

"Ben, for God's sake don't chase him away. I'm getting old. I couldn't run this place without him now. He really took hold."

Ben gestured briefly and went out. Pop sat shaking his head. A hardbitten old codger, Ben—one of the few real old-time peace officers left in the West.

The Antler Bar was a narrow hole-in-the-wall jammed in between an old adobe house and the back end of Sol Reed's Palace. Ben went in through the swinging doors, and the first man he saw was Staff, who was standing at the front end of the bar with his foot on the rail, having a quiet drink. Ben noted that he was not wearing guns. Come to think of it, he'd never seen a gun on him.

Ben went over and stood beside him. There was a ripple of comment in the crowded bar and Ben was pointed out to some strangers. "That old guy?" somebody said, and there were a few laughs.

Ben pretended not to hear.

"Buy you a drink, Mr. Gann," said Staff.

"All right," said Ben.

The bartender poured him a full one, then left the bottle on the bar. There was a brief silence as Ben turned the glass in his fingers.

"Your right name Stafford?" he asked, finally.

"Yes sir. William Stafford."

"Pop thinks pretty highly of you."

Staff glanced at the marshal, but said nothing.

"You see," said Ben, "we got a problem around here. Outlanders coming in from God knows where—strangers. You're one of them. Nobody knows anything about you."

Staff looked straight ahead into the bar mirror. "It's a free country, Marshal. As long as I behave myself, what's your objection?"

"My objection," said Ben, "is you're always talking to my daughter. I don't know you. She doesn't know you. It might cause gossip around the town."

The back of Staff's neck had turned red. "You got a point, Marshal," he said. "You really got a point. I'll try not to talk to her any more."

Ben had expected opposition, trouble. He turned and looked at Staff. "You mean it?"

"Yes sir," said Staff. "I mean it. She's a real fine girl and I wouldn't get her talked about for anything."

"Good," said Ben. "Well, that's settled."

"Of course, you understand, Marshal, it might be kind of hard for me to avoid her, and I'm sure as God not going to hurt her feelings for any man," Staff went on. "I mean, if I happen to run into her. But I'll make it as brief as possible. A man can always be in a hurry."

"I'd appreciate it," said Ben, curtly.

Now he tossed his drink down and turned toward the door. But suddenly his way was barred by a huge, drunken outlander. Ben looked at him calmly.

"They told me you was an old man, Marshal," said the big drunk, giggling. "But I didn't know you was this old. Hell, you're old as my pappy. Doggone if you ain't. I'm from way back in Missouri, I really am."

He was wearing a Colt .44 very low on his right hip, and his big meaty hand was dangling near it.

"You're drunk," said Ben. "Go away some place. Sleep it off."

The Missourian roared with laughter, then his face hardened. "I got a good mind to teach you a lesson, Pappy. Damn your eyes. Don't call me no drunk."

The big hand was near the gun-butt now. All at once the Missourian gave a loud "oof" and his head came forward sharply. A gun-barrel had been jammed into his belly and he couldn't figure out how it had happened. He hadn't even seen a shadow of motion from the marshal.

"I think I'll teach *you* a lesson," said Ben. "Turn around."

The Missourian obeyed without argument.

"Get down on your hands and knees."

The drunk hesitated, then turned and looked at Ben, his face showing fury.

"Do what I say," said Ben, "or you'll never get back to Missouri."

The big fellow dropped to his hands and knees, trying to ignore all the laughter and catcalls about him.

"Now crawl out," said Ben.

The man started to crawl.

"Shall I ride him over to Urbey's, Marshal?" called somebody.

But that was too much for the drunk. Rising abruptly to his haunches he tried to draw his gun and turn at the same time. Ben took one quick step and belted him over the head with his gun-barrel. The man fell forward with a loud groan and lay flat on his stomach, out cold.

With his elbows on the bar and a match between his teeth, Staff looked on in silence. His face was expressionless.

Ben turned. "Nolly! That you over there?"

A little bearded man piped up: "It's me, all right, Marshal."

"Go see if you can find Homer. I want this bum jailed."

"Yes sir, Marshal."

Ben turned back to the bar and motioned for the bottle. The bartender pushed it over to him. "Sorry, Ben," he said.

Ben shrugged. "What can you expect with all the trash coming in?"

The bar was quiet now. There was no more laughing at Ben's expense.

"Shall I pour some water over him, Marshal?" asked the bartender.

"Later," said Ben; then he turned to Staff. "Drink? On me this time."

"Why, thank you, Marshal," said Staff. "I believe I will."

III

It was a little after nine-thirty when Doc and his "boys" sauntered into Solomon Reed's Palace Saloon and Gambling Hall. They'd been "washed down and curried," as Doc said, and they hardly looked like the same three men who had ridden into San Ygnacio that day at sundown. Pinto was cleanly shaved and was wearing dark clothes and a string tie with his white shirt. Frenchy, also in black and white, had had his mustache and imperial trimmed, and his long, coarse black hair cut down to less barbarous dimensions. While Doc, as if it was his object to stand out from the others, was wearing a freshly pressed gray, Eastern-type suit, a wide, red silk stock with his soft white turn-down collar, and a dark-blue waistcoat with gilt buttons. Pinto and Frenchy wore one gun apiece, inconspicuously, while Doc did not seem to be armed at all, as he had a nickel-plated thirty-eight in a shoulder-holster and a fighting-knife sheathed in an inside coat pocket. His black Stetson looked brand-new, it had been brushed so thoroughly.

Near the entrance they stopped and looked about them at the big, crowded bar. Two huge chandeliers glimmered high over their heads, and the long mahogany bar, highly polished, gave off a ruddy shine from the reflection of the lights. There were four bartenders working against a glittering background of mirrors, massed bottles, and glasses. Girls in silk and sequins circulated, switching their short skirts and showing their well-filled silk stockings. There was a loud, wild hubbub of talk and clinking glassware.

Doc looked at his "boys" and winked. Frenchy chuckled and began to sing under his breath. Pinto stared open-mouthed. "Well, I never," he said. "Rich place. Golly."

Somebody near them let out a shriek and, before Doc could turn, a large blonde girl had him in her arms and was hugging him fiercely.

"Doc, Doc," she cried, "remember Tombstone? Millie? That's me."

Doc disentangled himself politely and then held Millie off at arm's-length and studied her. "My, you're getting to be a big girl, Millie," he said, smiling. "A real big girl, but too loud, Millie, too loud."

"Oh, I'm sorry, Doc." She was almost whispering now. "I don't mean to embarrass you."

Doc slipped her a bill. "You didn't see me, Millie. Understand, dear? I want to be the first to tell a certain party that Arthur Sprigge, M.D., is in San Ygnacio."

"Oh, sure, Doc," said Millie, then she looked about her quickly. "But you better hurry, darling. Half-a-dozen Tombstone girls are here—they'll spot you. And Pony Willis is right down there at the end of the bar, and Leo Trotter's in here some place."

Doc chuckled. "That's a queer thing," he said. "The road-company badmen got here before the star of the original cast."

Millie laughed piercingly, then she put her hand over her mouth. "I'm sorry. But you was always so funny, Doc, saying those bright remarks."

Pinto was tapping Doc on the shoulder. Doc glanced at him in irritation. "Doc, how about I get fixed up with Millie? She's a fine big girl."

"Later, later," said Doc, brushing him off. "We've got all night."

"Ah, baybee, *très belle*," said Frenchy, bowing to Millie. "Wan nice beeg *mamselle* for Franchy. No?"

"Parlez-vous, I'm sure," said Millie, giggling. Then to Doc: "Who are they?"

"They carry my guns," said Doc. "I'm too weak. My life's catching up with me. Look, Millie. Stop laughing for a second. Is Sol Reed here?"

"He should be."

"Where's his office?"

"You go through the gambling room," she explained, pointing toward a big arched doorway. "It's at the back. Just says office."

"Thanks," said Doc, bowing slightly. "And remember—you didn't see me. And if you hear rumors I'm here, kill 'em. But it's only a matter of a few minutes."

"All right, Doc, all right," said Millie, hugging him.

In his office, Sol Reed was just rising to go out into the gambling room. He paused to light a cigar, then he took out a pocket-comb and carefully combed his curly brown hair, of which he was very proud. Sol was a big man, with the narrow, anxious face of a small one. Sol was a worrier. He was also a bluffer and bully when he was certain he could get away with it, as with women. You would not guess this, however, at first meeting, as he had a rather pleasing professional façade, bland, smiling, attentive, friendly.

He put it on like a mask, and he was just getting ready to put it on for the patrons of the Palace, when the door opened and Doc walked in, followed by Pinto and Frenchy.

"Hi, Sol," cried Doc, advancing with his hand outstretched. "Well, well. Heard you were in town."

"Doc Sprigge!" gasped Sol, his face showing a touch of pallor.

Doc studied him with well-acted surprise. "Hell, Sol,"

31

he said, "aren't you glad to see an old pal? Remember Dodge? Why, we're old-timers, you and me."

Sol winced inwardly at the thought of the horrible mistake he'd made in Dodge. Sometimes he woke up in the middle of the night in a cold sweat thinking about it. He'd tried to get Doc murdered. "God, I must have been crazy," he thought.

"How are you, Doc?" he said, trying without success to adjust his mask.

"Why, I'm fine, Sol, fine. Thought you'd be glad to know I was in town, so I came right over, me and the boys. A man like you can always use the country's top dealer."

So that was it! Sol reached out and grasped the desk for support. To take Doc into your establishment was like taking a fox into a henyard. But what could he do? He hemmed and hawed. "Well, you see, Doc, at the present time—"

"Good," cried Doc. "I'll take the job. A hundred a night for the three of us. Frenchy is the best case-keeper in the West. And Pinto is the best lookout. A dead shot with either hand."

With a groan, Sol sank down into his chair. "But, Doc," he began, trying feebly to save himself from a fate that made him shudder to contemplate, "I don't know if—"

"Of course," said Doc, "if you weren't a good friend of mine, Sol, I might just declare myself in—say, for a third of the take." Now Doc slipped his fighting-knife deftly from an inside coat pocket and began to pare his nails. "But you know me, Sol—live and let live is my motto. Later, if I drag the business in, and I always do, we can raise the ante—or maybe you'll offer me a piece. Eh, Sol?"

Sol kept his eyes lowered. He did not want to see that murderous-looking knife, sharp as a razor, you could bet. Sol had a horror of a naked steel blade. But it was true what Doc said. With his reputation he always dragged in the business. People came in droves just to look at Doc. Tough gamblers wanted to match wits with the slickest and crookedest faro dealer west of the Mississippi. There was only one trouble. Doc always ended up killing somebody, or maybe three or four, sometimes a peace officer among them.

Sol couldn't bring himself to speak. But he knew it was useless to refuse. Of course he could go to the law. But how long could it protect him? With his eyes still lowered, he began slowly to nod his head.

"Good, fine," cried Doc, ostentatiously putting the knife away. "I knew you wouldn't go back on an old friend. We saw some real rough times in Dodge, didn't we, Sol, old boy?"

Sol kept nodding like a mechanical toy. Frenchy and Pinto exchanged stupefied glances. This was too easy for their taste. Much too easy. But then that knife of Doc's often did the trick. It was far better than words as a persuader. But, even so, most men weren't as chicken-hearted as this smooth-faced, curly-haired half-man slumping there in defeat before them. They noticed the rings on his thick fingers. They smelled the bay rum and the pomade. They wanted to kick him.

"Fine, fine," cried Doc, ignoring Sol's collapse. "Get a table ready. Tell it around the place. We'll start now."

Berta had finished her darning and sewing long ago and, in order to keep busy so the time would pass faster, she had changed the shelf papers in the kitchen cupboard and had taken care of a lot of other little odds and ends that accumulate about a house. Now she was looking for something else to do. It was after eleven o'clock and she was vaguely worried. Neither Ben nor Homer had been back since supper. This was very unusual, but she was certain she knew what it meant: trouble uptown, and a lot of it.

She picked up the newspaper and tried to read it. But, actually, reading of any kind bored her; she soon tossed the paper away, and sat listening to the night sounds and the erratic ticking of the little clock. The marshal's house was at the far southern end of the town, where Howard Street came to a deadend at Indian Road. All about were stores, closed for the night, and residences: no saloons, no gambling joints, no honky-tonk at all. Just north of the marshal's house was the old adobe jail. Around the corner on Indian Road was Judge Howard's house, and, beyond that, his offices and the one and only courtroom in San Ygnacio, where the judge sat on the bench every day unless he was occupied by city business in his capacity as mayor. It was very quiet in this pleasant corner of the town. The sounds from upper Howard Street, where almost all the night activity took place, were muffled and faint.

Berta felt herself nodding, and yet she didn't want to go to bed. She knew that as soon as she put her head on the pillow, her sleepiness would leave her and she'd lie listening and wondering, until either Homer or Ben "checked in," as they said, to see that she was all right.

She rose and began to walk about. Suddenly she remembered what Ben had said about her "pants." Was it true? Were they too tight? Hurrying into the bedroom, she quickly took off her dress and put on the jeans, then she brought the big lamp in from the sitting-room, put it on a table, and took down a large wall-mirror and placed it on the floor against the wainscoting. Now she turned her back to the mirror and looked into it over her shoulder. She was horrified. "Oh, my goodness," she said, aloud. And then she thought about Staff, and a flush mounted from her neck and rose up into her hair. She'd been wearing the jeans the first time she'd met him—at the corral; also in Boggs's general store, where they'd talked for such a long time . . . and where else? She took another look. "Oh, why didn't he tell me before?" she thought. Berta was still a kid in some ways. She was far less conscious of her body than most girls her age. "What'll Staff think of me?" she wondered, worrying. "Going around in those awful tight old jeans. Did he think I was trying to show myself off?" And then she was struck by a sudden thought and flushed again. "I'll bet that big man did. The one who tried to . . ."

She pulled the jeans off hastily and threw them on the floor of the closet, then she put on a new cotton dress she'd just bought, hung the mirror back on the wall, and began to experiment with her hair. "I just never paid much attention to myself, I guess," she thought. "Oh, I'm glad Ben said something, even if he was mean about it."

Now she tried her hair in a ladylike chignon, and laughed at herself in the mirror. Daintily holding up her skirts, she began to waltz about the room. "I wonder if Staff can dance," she thought. "His feet look awfully big—and I'm sure he's got bony knees." She giggled to herself, a little ashamed of her thoughts.

There was a sharp tap at the outer door. She hurried to answer it, forgetting the new dress and the chignon.

"It's me, Miss Berta. It's me," came Homer's plaintive voice. Someway, he sounded excited.

Berta opened the door wide, glad of any company, even Homer's. The deputy stared at her, openmouthed, and almost dropped his rifle.

"My golly, Miss Berta," he gasped, "but you sure look beautiful."

Berta glanced down at herself in surprise, then blushed. "I was just trying on my new dress, Homer."

"Golly," said Homer, coming in and leaving the door wide open. Suddenly he seemed to come to himself. "Marshal here?"

"No," said Berta. "Hasn't been back since supper. What's the matter uptown?"

"Oh, drunks," said Homer, disdainfully. "I jailed six.

35

Ben had to slam one pretty good. You should see the fellow—six foot four—and now sitting in his cell a-crying. Said we shouldn't ought to have hit him." Homer snickered sadly. "I guess I must have missed Ben some way uptown. Doggone it. I want him."

"Something wrong?"

Homer hesitated and then his lips began to work but no sound came out. Sometimes when Homer got very excited he stammered. Berta felt worried, but before she could ask any more questions, Luis Aranjo came hurrying around the corner of the house. His eyes were big. He looked startled.

"Homer," he called, panting for breath, "I came all the way down here from Mextown to tell the marshal . . . did you hear—?"

"Yes," said Homer. "Doc Sprigge. I'm looking for the marshal, too."

"Who is Doc Sprigge?" Berta demanded. "Why are you both so excited?"

"Well, Miss Berta—" Homer began, in his exasperatingly slow way.

Luis cut in impatiently. "He's the number-one gun in the West, since Hickok got killed. He's dealing faro as big as you please, up at Sol Reed's. Pete Lopez told me about it. I didn't believe it, so I went up to see for myself. Little man. Looks like a gentleman. Talks very polite."

"I got to go get a look," said Homer, eagerly.

"Better find the marshal first," warned Luis.

Homer's face fell. "Yes, you're right."

"Got two men with him," Luis went on. "One keeping cases, one in the lookout's chair. I'll bet there won't be any monkey business at that table."

Berta studied them both. "You mean he's wanted by the law, this doctor? That Ben will have to—?"

"We don't want him for anything," said Homer. "I guess as long as he behaves himself here . . . But that's up to the marshal. Right, Luis?"

"Right," said Luis. "We better go look for Ben." Luis

seemed a little nervous now. "If I know Ben, he'll want a word with Doc."

Berta hesitated, then said: "Will you—kind of—look after Ben? I know he doesn't need any looking after. But—"

"We will, Miss Berta, we will," said Homer; then his eyes wandered politely over her, from shoes to hair. "Doesn't she look beautiful, Luis, in that new dress and with her hair that way?"

Luis grinned in embarrassment. He was fat and out of it as far as Berta was concerned. "She sure does, Homer."

In a moment they gestured good-by and left. Berta closed the door thoughtfully. How Ben stood it, she didn't know. He was up till all hours; sometimes, on Saturday nights, he didn't put the town to bed till four a.m.; nevertheless, he was always at the kitchen table by seven, shaved and dressed, waiting for his breakfast. The whole thing was, Ben loved his work. Gloried in it.

Berta walked back to the bedroom, worrying about him.

Pop Urbey, who had plenty of money and could afford practically any kind of accommodations, slept on an army cot in a storeroom behind his office. Pop was alone now. His wife had died, and his sons had scattered toward far horizons. So Pop had sold his house and moved into the livery barn.

"I'll stay in no house alone, nor in a hotel room neither," he explained to anybody who would listen. "I'd get to talking to myself and worrying about my liver or something at night when I couldn't sleep. Here in the barn I got company. Night hostlers moving about. I can hear the horses stomping. And I like the smell. I was raised on an Indiana farm. Used to sleep in the barn in the summer. Good hay smell, horse smell. Makes me sleep like a top."

He was laughed at. People thought he was lying, to cover

up his parsimony. "That old Pop—tight as the bark on a tree," they'd say. "Heavy with money—and sleeps in the barn to save rent." Yet Pop was telling the truth.

But tonight Pop couldn't sleep. He was too excited. He'd heard the news. Doc Sprigge was dealing faro at the Palace. A lantern burned at Pop's feet, throwing out faint-rayed beams into the darkness. Pop kept scratching matches, lighting his cigar. "Doggone! What do you know about that!" he repeated over and over, to himself.

At about eleven thirty he heard somebody enter the office. One of the nightmen? But a chair squeaked and there was a thump. Somebody had sat down. Pop lay listening. The nightmen never sat in the office. Pop didn't allow it. Suddenly he had an idea.

"Staff!" he called. "That you?"

Now he heard the floorboards groan, and his door was opened.

"What's the matter, Mr. Urbey?" came Staff's polite voice. "Did I disturb you?"

"No, no," cried Pop. "Too excited to sleep. Come in, come in. Sit down."

Staff took off his hat and sat down on a box beside the lantern.

"I guess you haven't heard the news yet," crowed Pop, delighted to be the first one to tell Staff. "Biggest news in years."

"What's that?"

"Doc Sprigge's here. Dealing faro at the Palace."

Staff hesitated, then said: "Got a spot already, eh?"

There was something about the way Staff said this that made Pop wonder. "You knew he was here?"

"Yes," said Staff, after a brief hesitation. "*You* saw him."

Pop sat up abruptly. "Staff, have you been drinking? I never laid eyes on the man. I'd like to. Been hearing about him for ten-twelve years."

38

"He sold us the three horses, Mr. Urbey. You took care of the bills of sale."

Pop was stunned. "Good God! That little one who did the talking?"

"Yes," said Staff.

"Him?" Pop couldn't get over it. "Why, he'd hardly come up to my chin and he'd have to stand twice to make a shadow. Why didn't you tell me? Why didn't you tell me?" Pop got more and more excited.

"Well," said Staff, "I didn't think you'd care about a no-good murdering son of a bitch like that. So I didn't tell you."

There was a pause. Pop lay back, deflated. "Yes, Staff," he said, finally, "I guess you're right. But he's a famous man. Joe Ballard, that owns the gun store, came over with the news. Says Doc has killed thirty men on the frontier."

"Oh, those figures get upped," said Staff, mildly. "He's killed a few. No doubt about that."

There was a long pause. Suddenly a thought occurred to Pop that whetted his curiosity. "Staff," he said, "how did you know it was Doc?"

"Well," said Staff, "I saw him once down in Texas. I was around nineteen or twenty then. Must be eight-nine years ago. He was—well—he was pointed out to me."

"Did he look about the same?"

"Just the same," said Staff. "He almost got lynched down there later. A woman friend of his named Kate set a hotel on fire so he could escape. Deputies were holding him in the hotel to save him from a mob."

"What did he do?"

"Killed three men in a street fight."

"Why lynch him for that? Three to one."

"They were popular fellows in the town. Doc was considered a no-good bastard. So they decided to lynch him."

"That's not fair," spluttered Pop.

"Maybe not," said Staff. "But he was using a rifle against six-shooters."

"Makes it about even then," said Pop.

"I guess so," said Staff.

There was a long pause. Pop smoked thoughtfully. Staff seemed to just sit there, turning his hat in his hands.

"What you doing back, son?" asked Pop. "Glad to have you, of course. Just curious."

"Oh, I don't know," said Staff. "Restless. I live in Mextown, you know. Those Mexicans sing and play guitars a lot. Hell, I like this barn. I like the horses. Peaceful. A horse is a peaceful animal. Treat him right, he'll treat you right. Not like men."

"You spoke a true word there," said Pop. "My sentiments exactly. Why don't you put a cot in the office, Staff? Sleep here. Save rent."

"Oh, I don't want to put you out none, Mr. Urbey," said Staff. "I might be a nuisance."

"No, no," Pop protested. "Love to have you. We could talk at night when we couldn't sleep. I mean it, Staff."

"Okay," said Staff. "That suits me fine."

Pop sighed with contentment. He missed his sons. Goddamned no-good rascals—but he missed them just the same. Staff had been kind of like a son to him for sometime now. This sort of made it official.

Howard Street was crowded and noisy as the marshal, followed by Luis and Homer, made his way toward the entrance of the Palace. Many turned to look after him, nudging one another and whispering. Strangers, in from all points of the compass, and used to the sight of hulking young peace officers, were astounded by their first sight of the famous marshal of San Ygnacio. "Why, he's a skinny old man," they'd say, staring. "You mean to tell me that's Ben Gann?"

But Ben ignored the noise and the comment. He was dressed as usual—Berta never being able to smarten him up—in heavy-duty jean pants with a short jacket to match, a gray flannel shirt with no tie, old worn boots, and a black Stetson that was turning greenish with age. Two ivory-handled .45's swung low at his hips, the holsters tied to his thighs with thongs. His badge of office, pinned to the left side of his jacket, was no star, but a mere bar of metal, containing one word: Marshal.

In the tight jean pants his legs, slightly bowed, looked thin and old, but he walked vigorously.

When they reached the entrance, he turned to his deputies. "You boys wait here."

Luis nodded. But Homer's face showed disappointment. Ben's sharp eyes missed little, and he asked abruptly, "What's the matter with you, Homer?"

"Nothing, Marshal. Only I haven't seen him yet."

Ben's eyes flashed. "Oh, you haven't seen him yet. This is not a minstrel show or a circus, Homer. Stay here."

"Y-yes sir," stammered Homer.

A group of talking, laughing men were coming out of the Palace. Ben shouldered through them and disappeared. The men looked at each other, then they looked off at the two deputies, then they turned and went back into the Palace.

"Doggone, I don't know," said Homer, dubiously.

"What's the matter?" asked Luis.

"Couldn't he talk to him over in the hotel room later?"

Luis snorted scornfully. "The marshal wants to talk to him in public."

"Don't seem right," said Homer. "Just because he's a famous man. What's the marshal got against him as long as he behaves himself?"

Luis compressed his lips, made no further comment, and began to roll a cigarette. Homer shifted his rifle about awkwardly, then leaned it against the building. People were always laughing at Homer for his unorthodox equipment.

Why lug a rifle around all day long? And why wear a little .32, waist high and toward the front? Homer refused to explain when he was tackled. "It's just a habit I got," he'd say, grinning sheepishly.

"Sometimes I don't understand the marshal at all," grumbled Homer, reaching for his makings.

"You don't need to," said Luis. "Just do what he says. That's good enough for me."

Inside, Doc, dealing to a crowded table, began to notice a hubbub in the place, a hubbub with unusual overtones. He glanced over at Pinto in the lookout's chair, and Pinto quickly rubbed his chin and raised one finger significantly, as if pointing. In a moment, Ben Gann moved into the circle of the players and stood looking down at Doc.

"Hold the deal," said Doc, then he rose, smiling. "Well for God's sake," he cried, "Ben Gann."

Ben had his thumbs hooked in his gun-belt. Doc swung his right hand toward him as if to shake hands, but, seeing at once that the hand would be refused, he continued the gesture to the upper lefthand pocket of his coat and took out a stogie, bit off the end and lit up, as he continued to speak.

"Haven't seen you for—how long is it, Ben?"

The marshal just stood looking at him grimly.

"Years, anyway," Doc went on, cheerfully. "You look about the same, maybe a little older. Same guns, I see."

"How long you figuring to stay, Doc?" asked Ben, cutting in.

The players had all stepped back, and now they were in a rough semicircle about the two men. The big room was very quiet. Play had even been halted at the other tables.

"Oh, you know me," said Doc. "Here today and gone tomorrow."

"By request, usually," snapped the marshal.

"Ben," said Doc, laughing, "don't be so tough on an old friend. I've had my troubles, yes. A man has to defend himself. You know me, Ben. Live and let live."

Ben merely stared at him grimly, then he studied Pinto and Frenchy in silence for a moment. Pinto showed no expression at all, but the eyelid of his pink eye twitched nervously. Frenchy rose from his chair and bowed.

"Bon soir, m'sieu," he said. "Eet is pleasure to meet wiz the so famoos marshal. I 'ave hear *beaucoup* about heem."

"Where did you get this pretty pair, Doc?" asked Ben.

"Oh, they attached themselves to me, one way or another," said Doc.

After a short silence, Ben said: "Never could understand you, Doc. Educated man like you, graduate doctor. You should be patching people up, not filling them with holes."

Nobody laughed except Doc. "Well, I'll tell you, Ben," said Doc, "it's a long story, but I'll make it brief. I patched people up till I found out they weren't worth the trouble, then I started filling them with holes."

A ripple of laughter now ran around the semicircle. Ben ignored it. "Doc," he said, "I'd prefer to have you move on."

The room had become silent again. Some of the men began to press slowly back away from the table.

"I may do that," said Doc, smiling. "When I'm ready."

"I'm not telling you when to go," said Ben. "I'm just the marshal of San Ygnacio. That's my only job. You're just a stranger here as far as I'm concerned. I have no reason—yet—to jail you or run you out. I'm just saying what I'd prefer."

"It's good to be frank," said Doc, carelessly. "So I'll say what *I* prefer. I prefer to stay, Ben—till further notice."

"All right," said Ben. "But let me say this. I'll never give you the benefit of the doubt, Doc. If there's trouble, and there always is with you, out you go—on your feet or on your back, as you prefer."

Doc laughed. "Ben," he said, slowly, "I never try to predict the future. But let's put it this way: I've never gone out on my back yet."

"There's always a first—and last—time," said Ben. Then he ran his eyes over Doc, Pinto, and Frenchy, hesitated, then turned and went out through the jam of men crowding round the table. They made way for him respectfully.

Doc was just resuming his seat when something caught his eye off to his right. He rose quickly, hurried through the crowd, and intercepted Sol Reed, who seemed to be moving with undue haste in the direction of the disappearing marshal. Sol started at the sight of the little doctor emerging from the crowd, and stopped.

"Where are you going?" asked Doc, abruptly.

"Well, I—I—uh—thought I ought to pay my respects to Marshal Gann. He hardly ever comes in here and—"

"Go back to your office and stay there," said Doc. "And if you ever tell Ben Gann that I forced my way in here, I'll kill you."

Sol's face turned chalk-pale. Doc's slitted eyes were almost closed. His mouth was twisted to one side, his teeth showing in a snarl that was like that of a dangerous dog.

"But, Doc," Sol protested, raising his hands feebly, "I had no intention of—"

"No, you had no intentions of—you crooked bastard," snarled Doc. "What about Dodge? You think I'll ever forget that? Don't try anything like that again or I'll carve you up like a side of beef."

Sol winced. Doc turned on his heel and went back to the table.

It was after four a.m. when Doc, Pinto, and Frenchy left the Palace and started for the Long Horn Hotel, across the street. Both Pinto and Frenchy were worrying about Doc. He'd been his usual sparkling self till about three o'clock and then, all of a sudden, he'd got irritable and had ranted at Frenchy for making mistakes keeping the cases. And then he'd ranted at Pinto for nodding in the lookout's chair. In both instances, Doc had been wrong. Frenchy had not made any mistakes. Pinto hadn't nodded.

Could it have been the marshal's visit? If so, why had Doc waited hours to show a reaction? They were deeply puzzled and uneasy.

At the Long Horn, they had a big corner room on the front. Pinto and Frenchy slept in a huge double bed; Doc across the room in a single. Nobody said anything as they began to undress. Suddenly Doc flung one of his boots across the room and it landed with a crash against the wainscoting. Pinto and Frenchy, who had their backs turned, jumped.

"Don't know what's the matter with me," yelled Doc. "Must be getting old. Memory's going. Can't remember a damned thing any more."

Pinto and Frenchy looked at each other in consternation.

"What is it, Doc?" asked Pinto, cautiously.

Doc slapped his forehead irritably. "It's that fellow at the corral. I know him as well as I know you. And yet I can't remember who he is or where I met him."

"The fellow at the corral—?" Pinto began, vaguely. "Oh, yeah." Then he laughed. "Frenchy and me was getting worried about you, Doc. You been raising hell all over the place. We thought maybe the marshal—"

"That old fool," said Doc, laughing suddenly. "He's getting so old his eyes are fading. Know what I mean? You can tell a man's age from his eyes. It's even surer than his hands. He's old as hell. No—he don't worry me at all. It's that fellow at the corral. He's a gun. Mark my word. He's a gun, and a big one. And I can't for the life of me—" Doc broke off and sat staring across the room. "Now wouldn't that curl your hair?"

Frenchy, stripped to his long underwear, shrugged. "Why worry, Doc? What's the difference?"

"Why, you numbskull," yelled Doc, "a man never

45

knows where trouble's coming from. When I'm in a town I always know the guns, all about them, you might say, then I know where I stand, how to handle things. Now this fellow's a gun. But I can't remember a thing about him, and so I can't figure how he'll operate, if there's trouble." Doc regarded his two "boys" for a moment in silence. "I guess you wouldn't understand. You just go stumbling around, grace of God. It's a miracle you both weren't planted long ago."

After a pause, Pinto said: "Maybe he just looks like this fellow, Doc."

Frenchy expected an outburst, but Doc merely sighed and nodded. "I've thought about that. Could be. I doubt it. But it could be."

"He don't wear guns," said Pinto.

"That's right," said Doc.

"Would a top gun go around naked?"

"If he was hiding, he might," said Doc. "Just to throw people off. Oh, hell—let's go to bed. The sun will be up before long and she'll get noisy in the streets."

So they put out the lamp and went to bed. In a few moments, both Frenchy and Pinto were snoring. But Doc lay on his back with his hands under his head, staring up at the ceiling. He saw the windows lighten with dawn. He heard the roosters crowing in the Mexican settlement. He heard the freight wagons rolling by, on their way to the railroad spur, far across the mile-high tableland. Finally he slept.

IV

It was a beautiful spring morning several days later; the sun was warm, there wasn't a cloud in the sky, and a cool, gentle breeze was blowing up from the south, bringing a pleasant odor of dew-drenched, desert vegetation.

Berta was moving briskly along the sunny side of the street, on her way to the post office. She was wearing a pretty, fresh-looking cotton dress and her red hair was up in a large bun.

"Hi, Miss Berta," somebody called, as she started across the intersection of Howard and San Juan.

She turned, and found herself confronted by a grinning old man. His beard was grizzled, his clothes patched and worn, but clean. Mule Casper, the desert rat and prospector, still, after thirty years, looking hopefully for El Dorado.

"Hello, Mr. Casper," said Berta, smiling at him.

"Just got in," said Mule. "Laws, what's happening to this town? Even you've changed, Miss Berta. Where's them tight pants?" Mule guffawed.

Berta felt herself flushing and looked about her quickly to see if anybody had overheard. Two men, standing at the corner, had. They guffawed with Mule.

"It's about time I grew up, don't you think, Mr. Casper?" asked Berta, politely, although she felt like slapping the old man.

"I don't know," said Mule. "I sure liked them pants."

The two men guffawed again. Berta smiled rather stiffly at old Mule, then hurried on across the street and into a big old adobe building on the corner, which housed not only the post office, but the stagecoach office and waiting-room, and Wells Fargo.

She felt overheated and irritable. Old men were such a trial sometimes. Why had he talked so loudly? Why had he insisted about the pants? Good thing Ben wasn't around. There would certainly have been some sparks. "How could I have been so careless?" she kept asking herself. "I just had no idea that men were so—!" She broke off and tried to dismiss the subject from her mind.

"Morning, Miss Berta."

She gave a start. Staff! He was standing there—his eyes showing surprise—smiling at her, with a stack of letters in his hand. He had his big hat off. She didn't like his hat. The rim was pushed up so far on the sides that it looked like a boat. Now she noticed for the first time how fine in texture his light-brown hair was and how short it was cut. Smiling, he looked both boyish and older than his years. There were deep squint-wrinkles at the outer corners of his eyes. It was a kind of weariness or tiredness, she decided, feeling a sudden rush of sympathy.

"Oh, good morning, Staff," she said, hurriedly. "I wasn't looking where I was going. I almost ran you down."

"I—uh—I just come for Mr. Urbey's mail," said Staff. "Well, I'll be on my way."

He put his hat on, smiled, bowed slightly, and went out, hurrying past Berta as if afraid she might try to detain him. Berta looked after him, hurt. He might at least have stopped for another word or two. She just couldn't understand it. He'd always seemed so friendly before. But—of course, there was his work—and maybe Mr. Urbey waiting for his mail. Although she wouldn't admit it to herself, her whole morning was spoiled.

Her lips were trembling slightly as she went to the window for her mail. Mr. Burke, clerk and assistant postmaster, greeted her politely but with a touch of banter in his voice.

"My, you're getting to be quite a lady, Miss Berta," he said. "I hardly know you. Here you are. The marshal's mail. And how's the marshal on this fine sunny day?"

Berta had to force herself to speak. She felt depressed. "Oh, he's fine."

"Terrible job he's got. Terrible," said Mr. Burke. Suddenly he cried out: "Wait a minute. Is that tall fellow from Pop's still here?"

"Staff? No. He's gone," said Berta, flushing slightly.

"There's another letter here for Pop," said Mr. Burke. "Got mixed into *your* mail someway. I guess it's just not my— Oh, well; he can get it tomorrow."

Berta hesitated briefly; then she said: "I'd be glad to take it over to Mr. Urbey." Immediately she felt guilty, remembering what Ben had said to her about Staff and getting herself talked about, and all. But surely there was nothing wrong in taking a letter to Mr. Urbey!

"Why, that's mighty nice of you," said Mr. Burke. "Here it is. Mighty nice of you. I like that dress. Got a new beau or something, Miss Berta? You sure are primped up."

Mr. Burke was very talkative. She had quite a time trying to get away from the window without hurting his feelings.

As Berta stepped into the livery-barn office she suppressed a quick look of dismay. Mr. Urbey was alone. He was sitting at his desk, smoking a cigar, and reading his mail.

"Well, Berta," he cried, looking up in surprise, then rising. "Glad to see you. How are you, child, how are you?"

"Please sit down, Mr. Urbey," said Berta; then she explained the reason for her visit and handed him the letter.

And while she was talking it suddenly struck her that she had done something foolish. Mr. Urbey would be sure to tell Ben that she'd been over to see him, and Ben had warned her plainly not to go to the corral any more. She knew Ben well. The delivery of the letter would seem like a mere subterfuge to him—which, actually, it was, although Berta was not quite ready to admit that to herself. "It's only neighborly," she thought. But she became very nervous, and turned to leave.

"Here, here," said Pop. "You going to run off like that? It's hot today. You must be warm, child. Sit down for a minute. I hardly ever get to see you. If I know Ben he keeps you home and off the street pretty much, eh? Ben's a very strict fellow. Too strict for his own good, maybe, sometimes." She seemed to be hesitating. "Sit down, Berta. You're not in that much of a hurry."

Berta sat down and fussed with her skirt. Pop resumed his seat behind the desk, puffed on his cigar, and smiled at her benignly. Real pretty young'un! None of that hawknosed Ben about her. A cute little nose that turned up just enough. Must take after the other side of the family. Though, come to think of it, Ben's hair had been sandy, almost red, before it had turned gray.

Just as Berta was about to speak, Staff came in with an old saddle and a handful of harness. He stared blankly.

Pop laughed. "Big surprise, eh, Staff? A pretty, red-haired girl so early in the morning." Then he explained about the letter.

Staff tossed the saddle and harness into a corner, took off his hat, and said: "Too bad you were put to that trouble, Miss Berta. Thank you."

"Oh, I don't mind," said Berta, staring down at her hands.

"Sit down, Staff, sit down," said Pop. "Let's have a nice

visit with Berta. If you leave, she'll leave. She don't want to talk to old fat Pop—and I like company, especially the company of young'uns, since my three boys lit out."

"You're wrong, Mr. Urbey," said Berta. "I like to talk to you and visit with you."

Staff shifted about uncomfortably, not knowing whether to go or stay. Pop chuckled. "Oh, yes?" he said. "Seems to me I shamed you into staying. Staff, will you sit down!"

Staff cleared his throat, sat down, and put his hat beside him on the floor. There was a brief silence, and Staff took out his makings, hesitated, then started to put them away.

"It's all right, Staff," said Pop. "Smoke. Berta doesn't mind."

Now Berta looked at Staff for the first time. "Oh, no. I don't mind," she said. "Ben smokes all the time around the house and so do Luis and Homer."

Staff looked at her thoughtfully. "Those are the deputies—Luis and Homer?"

"Yes," said Berta. "But they are more like members of the family. Eat supper with us every night."

"Lucky fellows," said Pop. "A pretty girl to eat with every night, and not only that—Ben told me you were a wonderful cook."

Berta's lips parted in surprise. "Ben told you that?"

"He sure did," said Pop. "He's a mighty stiff-necked old geezer but he's proud of his daughter, as he should be, eh, Staff?"

"Yes sir, Mr. Urbey. He should be," said Staff, smiling at Berta.

She was deeply pleased, not only by the sincerity in Staff's voice, but also because Ben had been talking about her to Mr. Urbey and was "proud" of her. At home Ben wouldn't let on. Never showed any affection. Grunted at her. Grumbled at her. Sometimes shouted at her.

"Say," said Pop to Staff, "show Berta how you can roll a cigarette with one hand."

"No," said Staff, flushing slightly. "She wouldn't be interested in that."

"Oh, but I would," said Berta. "I surely would."

So Staff showed her how it was done. Berta sat with her lips parted, watching. She had never in all her life seen such nimble fingers. It was almost like magic.

As Staff, still slightly embarrassed, was lighting up, Pop said: "Oh, he's an amusing fellow, Staff is; just full of tricks. Show her what you can do with a fifty-cent piece."

Staff wagged his head. "Pop, I ought to be out working. Miss Berta is not interested—"

"Oh, but I am," said Berta. "Please."

"Don't know if I got fifty cents," said Staff, and they all laughed.

He searched his pockets in vain. "Must be in my coat," he said.

Pop tossed him a half-dollar and Staff went to work with it. He made it disappear into thin air and return, to walk across his fingers as if it were alive, to move erratically from hand to hand, and then to go away altogether and finally reappear at the back of his neck.

Berta, her face flushed, kept laughing and clapping her hands.

"Did you ever see the like!" Pop exclaimed finally. "I swear it's uncanny."

"Oh, my goodness," cried Berta. "How did you ever learn to do that?"

"Well," said Staff, giving an embarrassed laugh, "used to have a lot of time on my hands out on the ranch. So . . . it was just for amusement, make the time pass."

"Look what he taught me," said Pop, picking up a pencil and balancing it on his fingers and moving it in such a way that it seemed to be made of rubber, bending eccentrically.

"Is that a regular pencil?" asked Berta, amazed.

"Yes," said Pop; then he handed the pencil across to Staff. "Show her. It's easy and it makes people's eyes bug."

Staff demonstrated how the trick was done and Berta watched eagerly, leaning forward. Finally she sank back. "Oh, I could never do that."

"Sure you could, Miss Berta," said Staff. "Here. Try it."

He gave her the pencil. She tried and tried but the pencil remained a pencil, with no illusion of a bend whatsoever.

"I told you I couldn't," said Berta.

"Show her, Staff, show her," called Pop, exasperated. "Take her hand and show her. That's the way you showed me. She won't bite you."

Staff hesitated, but Berta was smiling at him, and even offering her hand, so he placed the pencil on her fingers in the correct way and then, moving her hand with his own, demonstrated how to make her fingers limp, which was the basis of the illusion.

"You've got it. You've got it," cried Pop, hitting the desk.

Berta looked up quickly at Staff. As he'd been holding her hand, a current of emotion had passed between them and they were both aware of it. Staff leaned back away from her abruptly.

Berta gave a little hysterical laugh. "See, Mr. Urbey? I can do it. I can do it."

There was a sudden applause from the doorway and they all looked off in surprise. Doc, in his gray suit, was smiling at them.

Pop's jaw dropped. Staff got quickly to his feet, pushing back his chair with an automatic movement of his leg that didn't escape Doc. Berta merely looked at the dapper little man pleasantly.

"Am I intruding?" asked Doc, smiling.

"Miss Berta was just going," said Staff, quickly. "Weren't you, Miss Berta?"

Berta glanced up at Staff in surprise. But somehow it wasn't Staff at all. Or not the Staff she was used to. His face looked drawn, his eyes hard. "Why, yes," she said, rising. "I've got so many errands."

Staff escorted her past Doc and to the big entrance door. "What's the matter?" she inquired.

"He's not the kind of company for you, Miss Berta." Then he hesitated and finally went on hurriedly: "Nor am I."

Before Berta could question him, he turned abruptly and went back toward the office. She stood watching him go. She was bewildered—after the warmth of their hands together, the look in his eyes as he helped her with the pencil trick—why, suddenly, had he said such a thing to her?

She started off hurriedly toward Howard Street, looking about her rather guiltily. If she'd happen to run into Ben— well, she'd have some tall explaining to do. On Howard east of San Juan there were no stores of any kind; only Mexican houses, American bars, cantinas, and the big corral. She would just have no excuse for being there.

Doc was sitting across from Pop now, calmly smoking a stogie. Staff stood with his back to the office wall, his legs crossed and his arms folded.

"I didn't know you were the famous Doc Sprigge when you sold me the horses," Pop was saying. "I didn't know, in fact, till Staff told me that night."

Doc glanced at Staff. "Know me?"

"It was all over town," said Staff.

Pop was about to make a comment on this remark but a look from Staff deterred him. Pop coughed loudly and cleared his throat to cover up the fact that he'd almost pulled a bonehead play. That is, he tried to cover it up. But very little ever got past Doc.

"Just thought I'd drop by and pay my respects," said Doc. "And have a word with your helper here."

Staff said nothing. His face was expressionless.

"With Staff?" asked Pop, surprised. "Why?"

"Well, he honored me last night with his presence at my faro bank."

"That so?" said Pop, glancing at Staff.

"Yes," said Doc. "He played about ten or fifteen minutes then left. I'm just curious to know why. Was there some objection to my dealing, Staff?"

"No," said Staff. "I'm short of dough. I lost two or three times so I quit."

"I take it you won't be back."

"It's not likely."

Doc laughed. "Why don't you level with me, boy? You were just curious to see how badly I was cheating them. Right?"

"You're telling it," said Staff.

Doc turned to Pop. "You may think you've got a plain corral manager here, Mr. Urbey, but you're wrong. You've got something else. What—I don't know yet."

"That so?" said Pop, mildly.

"Very plausible fellow," said Doc. Then he turned to Staff. "I ought to know you, but somehow I don't. This bothers me."

"My name's William Stafford," said Staff. "I was born in Kansas. You must have me mixed up with somebody, Doc. And it would please me very much if you'd make up your mind to that fact."

Doc looked at Staff for a long time. Staff's eyes were bleak. In a moment Doc rose and smiled. "Maybe you're right," he said. "Yes, I'm sure you're right. A case of mistaken identity. So we'll say no more about it."

"I'd appreciate it," said Staff, his voice so cold that Pop turned to look at him in surprise.

Doc smiled and bowed in Pop's direction. "Your servant, Mr. Urbey. It's been a pleasure." Doc nodded to Staff and went out. Before either of them could speak, he put his head back in.

"Stafford, tell me something. Why were you so anxious to get that charming young lady out of here?"

"It's pretty obvious," said Staff.

There was a pause, then Doc laughed. "Now how do you suppose an old goat like Ben Gann ever happened to have a daughter like that? Morning, gents."

He left for good. Pop stared at Staff in surprise. "Now how did he know—?"

Staff shrugged. "Saw her on the street. Asked about her. Doc's interested in women—though not women like Miss Berta, as a rule. Women like the one who set the hotel on fire and could handle guns like a man. Besides, Doc likes to know everything. Never can tell when some little bit of information might come in handy. Oh, he's a real bastard, Mr. Urbey."

"H'm," said Pop. "And looks like a little gentleman. Wasn't even armed."

"Oh, he was armed, all right, Mr. Urbey," said Staff. "Shoulder-holster, probably; and he's always got a knife. He couldn't afford to go around unarmed. Too many men would like to kill him."

Pop glanced at Staff thoughtfully. "Who do you suppose he thinks you are?"

"I don't know. But I hope I cooled him off about that. It could get right annoying."

Staff stooped down and began to gather up the saddle and the harness.

"Let me say this," said Pop. "Whoever you are, it's all right with me."

"Thank you, Mr. Urbey," said Staff, swallowing, and speaking in an odd voice. "Thank you very much." Then he went hurriedly into the little side storeroom, lugging the equipment.

Pop sat smoking thoughtfully.

* * *

Doc had breakfast at the hotel, then he went back up to his room. Frenchy and Pinto were still snoring. Doc listened to the duet for a moment, then he slammed the door violently. Both men sat up with a start and stared in surprise as they saw Doc standing in the middle of the room, laughing at them.

"What time is it, Doc?" asked Pinto.

"About nine o'clock."

"Good God," exclaimed Pinto, and Frenchy groaned and lay back.

"I was down talking to that fellow at the corral," said Doc. "He's hiding out. Don't think he'll be any trouble."

"Good," said Pinto, yawning.

"Got a real cold eye on him," Doc went on. "I sure wish I could place him, not that it matters too much now. He's got his own problems, including the marshal's daughter."

Now Frenchy sat up. "The marshal's daughter! How do you know—?"

"I know everything," said Doc. "All a man's got to do is keep his eyes open. You're both too stupid for that. Something's got to come up and hit you."

"What's this about the marshal's daughter?" asked Pinto.

"Oh, he was teaching her a cute little trick with a pencil," said Doc, then he took a penholder from the writing desk and demonstrated. He had the trick down pat, after having seen it once.

Frenchy and Pinto were fascinated. They jumped out of bed and in a few minutes they were fighting over the penholder. Doc watched them sardonically for a while, but finally the uproar began to irritate him, so he snatched the penholder away and told them to get back into bed and shut up, he was going to take a nap till dinnertime, at noon.

"Aw, Doc," Pinto protested, "just when I was getting the hang of it.

* * *

Judge Howard was having supper with the marshal and his "family." Homer and Luis, very much in awe of him, ate in silence, and seemed to be trying to efface themselves. Ben chewed lustily—he still had most of his teeth—and stared off across the room, lost in thought. Berta had seated the judge next to her and they talked and laughed together as the meal progressed.

"You don't know what a treat for me this is, Ben," said the judge, finally. "Mrs. Gomez is a mighty fine cook and all that, but I get tired eating alone. Company is the best sauce."

This expressed Berta's sentiments exactly and she smiled at him. Ben merely grunted.

"Yes sir," the judge went on, trying to get Ben's attention, "and you've got a jewel of a girl here, Ben. I hope you appreciate that fact."

Ben turned and looked at the judge. "She's just a girl. I raised her. I ought to know."

Homer flushed with annoyance, but kept his eyes on his plate.

"Come on now, Ben," said the judge, laughing. "You don't fool me one bit. You know Berta's one in a thousand, and you're proud as Punch."

"Oh, Berta's all right," said Ben. "Always gets the pies too brown. But she's all right. Her mother was a better cook. And better looking."

"Don't you pay any attention to him," said the judge, turning to Berta. "I happen to know what he thinks about you. He told me, in an unguarded moment."

Both Luis and Homer glanced up quickly at the marshal. What would he say to that?

"What are you trying to do, Judge," asked Ben, "turn her head? That's pretty easy to do with a female."

The judge laughed. "Not Berta," he said. "She's very sensible."

Ben grunted. "No female is sensible. It's the wrong word

58

to apply to them. Smart, yes; but not sensible. How about some more coffee, Berta?"

Berta rose, patted him on the back, and went to the kitchen for the coffee-pot. Homer and Luis had finished their pie. They pushed back their chairs and began to make their excuses, because of the presence of the judge. Ben cut them off.

"Better be on your way, boys," he said. "It's a Saturday night and the trouble will likely start early. I'll be uptown shortly."

" 'By, Miss Berta," called Homer. "Wonderful supper."

Berta called good-by from the kitchen, and Homer and Luis went out.

The judge offered Ben a cigar, but Ben refused and got out an old corncob pipe. They sat smoking in silence for a moment. Finally the judge said: "You got a couple of good boys there, Ben."

Ben nodded. "Good boys. Do what I tell 'em."

"I took on a couple of new employees myself, today," said the judge, looking down at the ash on his cigar.

Ben glanced at him in surprise. "That so?"

"Well, the way the work's piling up," said the judge, "I had no alternative. Clerks."

"Oh," said Ben. "Do I know them?"

"Yes. Rufe Caton—that's Ed's boy. And Len Cline."

Ben nodded. "Good boys. Never any trouble. Belong here. But—clerks? That's a couple of pretty handy all-around boys, Judge."

"I didn't have much choice," said the judge, still looking at his cigar. "Len's got some education, you know. I'll just have to be patient with Rufe. He can write and cipher. That's about all. But he'll learn."

There was a long silence. The judge glanced up. Ben was studying him. "Do they figure to wear guns?" asked the marshal, finally.

"That's up to them," said the judge, shifting about

uncomfortably. "But sitting around an office—I wouldn't think—"

"Judge," said Ben, "I'm sure you mean well and all like that, but I don't want any interference from these boys."

The judge began to protest, but Ben went right on: "I can handle San Ygnacio. I may be getting old, but I'm far from feeble. My father could do a good day's work in the fields when he was eighty, and I am just like him."

"Listen, Ben," said the judge, deciding to come out into the open, "I'm not doubting your ability in the least. But you've got to face the facts. San Ygnacio's growing out of all recognition. You can't be every place. If I were you, I'd seriously consider putting on some extra men, myself; maybe even three or four."

"Do you want my badge?" snapped Ben.

The judge recoiled and waved a placating hand. "Ben, Ben; you're just not thinking straight. We wouldn't know what to do without you around here. You know that."

"Then let me handle things my own way," said Ben bluntly. Now he turned and looked over his shoulder. "Where in thunder is that coffee?"

Pushing his chair back abruptly, he went out to the kitchen. The pot was on the stove, warming; but Berta was paying no attention to it. She was standing by the sink doing something with a pencil, something idiotic, it seemed to Ben.

"What in thunder—!" he shouted.

Berta started, and turned to him, flushing. "I was just—"

"What's this nonsense with the pencil?" snapped Ben.

"It's a trick I learned," said Berta. "Look. I'll show you, Ben."

Her father snorted. "Tricks! What imbecile has been teaching you tricks with a pencil? Homer, no doubt. Bring the coffee."

He turned and went back into the dining-room.

Berta felt embarrassed that Ben had caught her "fooling

60

around," as he would have said, but also she felt warm, and young, and alive. Staff and his tricks! As she went to the stove to get the coffee-pot, she suddenly recalled what he'd said as he'd turned away from her: "Nor am I." What could he have meant? What was wrong with him? Nothing that she could see. Was he just too modest? And then there came into her mind a picture of Staff in the post office, with his hat off, smiling, but also looking a little worried, too. Why had he hurried away from her so fast? "That must be it," thought Berta. "He's just too modest. After all, he's only a sort of glorified hostler and he didn't even seem to have fifty cents—as if *I* cared!"

She carried the coffee-pot into the dining-room, where Ben and the judge were sitting at the table in silence. As she poured the coffee, she glanced from one to the other. The silence worried her. Now the judge looked up and shrugged slightly. So the judge had braced Ben and got nowhere!

She and the judge had talked it over that afternoon. The judge had been invited for a purpose. Apparently he'd failed to make a dent in Ben's armor. She sat down with a sigh, and sipped her coffee. The silence went on.

V

The Palace was roaring. The bar was lined three deep, a four-piece orchestra was playing in a corner, and at the far end of the big room, beyond the bar, a space had been cleared for dancing, and the girls were being whirled around energetically by booted males who were making a terrific clatter. Loud laughter rang out all over the bar. Although it was Saturday night and jammed to the walls, and hard liquor had been flowing for hours, everybody seemed happy and good-natured.

But in the gambling room things were different. Pony Willis emerged from it shaking his head, then stopped and ran his eyes along the crowded bar, trying to locate his pal, Leo Trotter. Finally he spotted him, dancing at the back with the big blonde girl from Tombstone. What was her name? Millie? With his thumbs hooked in his gun-belt, Pony strolled back along the bar and finally caught Leo's eye. Leo cavorted for a while longer, then he gave Millie a big hug and some money, and worked his way over to where Pony was standing at the end of the bar.

"What's the matter?" asked Leo, shifting his gun-belt around to a more comfortable position.

"There's going to be trouble," said Pony. "Doc! Let's mosey over to Mextown and sit ourselves down in a cantina for a quiet drink."

"Hell, I'm having too much fun," said Leo. "It's almost like Tombstone—and no goddamn Earps to worry about."

"Look," said Pony, "we been getting by fine here. If there's trouble, I want to be a long ways off till it cools down."

"Hell, I want to stay here with Millie," said Leo. "She's one helluva girl. But what's going on?"

"There's a big guy at the table giving Doc a bad time. Texan, I think. Doc's reputation don't seem to faze him. He's been warned by half-a-dozen men. He just laughs. First, he knocked the counters off and Doc called him. Then he puts up a howl that the case-keeper is not keeping cases honest—which, of course, he ain't—and Doc has to call him again. He won't go away. Keeps playing. Leo, if I know Doc, he'll blow up shortly—and this Texan will be *carried* away."

"Sure are some foolish men in this world," said Leo, thoughtfully. "Okay, Pony. Maybe you're right. Let's get out of here."

The two "road-company badmen," formerly of Tombstone, didn't even stop for another drink, but hurried out into the cool, dry, dusty air of Howard Street and started off north toward the Mexican settlement.

In the gambling room, the atmosphere was very tense, and some men, like Leo and Pony, wanting no part of a shooting scrape, began to drift out into the bar and then out onto the street. Word was gradually getting around that there might be trouble, and now men of a different type began to sidle into the gambling room from the bar, moving cautiously, ready to duck or hit the floor, but not wanting to miss any of the excitement.

At the moment things were quiet at Doc's table as he dealt. Pinto, in the lookout's seat, seemed to be lazily, even sleepily, regarding things; and Frenchy at the far end of the table hummed to himself as the cards were turned and he noted them down, keeping track of which had been played and which had not. The big Texan was gambling now in surly silence. Earlier he'd informed everybody that he was called Wilfred and that if there was any man in the place who didn't like that name, or thought it sissy, said man could draw and go to shooting. Nobody drew. Doc, with a stogie clamped in the corner of his mouth, and looking as dapper as usual in his gray suit, flipped the cards from the box deftly.

"Deuce wins," he said in a monotonous professional voice. "King loses."

"That goddamned king," muttered Wilfred. "Ain't he been up afore? Hey, case-keeper?"

"Non, non, m'sieu," called Frenchy.

"Don't gimme that spig talk," cried Wilfred. "Talk American, for Christ's sake."

Wilfred was ignored. The game went on.

"Trey wins," said Doc. "Ten loses."

"Ain't I seen that red ten afore?" asked Wilfred. "What's going on here? Why, where I come from they hang crooked faro hucksters."

A gasp traveled round the room. Doc turned the box over.

"This table's closed for the time being," he said.

"Oh, no, you don't," cried Wilfred. "I lost my money here and I'm going to win it back. Set them cards up again."

"Mister," said Doc, "if you don't quiet down—"

But Doc never finished what he was going to say. Wilfred had whipped out his righthand gun and was holding it on Doc. "Set 'em up again," he yelled.

Doc moved so fast that most of the men in the place didn't know what had happened until it was explained to them later. They heard Wilfred give a sort of wild scream; a gun went off and they heard a bullet go through the faro table with a sound as of a nail being pulled out by the roots; they saw Wilfred stagger blindly, they saw his pants fall down, and then with astonishment, they saw him follow the pants to the floor where he writhed and kicked for a moment, then turned over on his stomach, gave a loud despairing groan and lay still.

"What happened? What happened?" the men cried.

Old Mule Casper had seen the whole thing and was chuckling to himself. "Why, Doc split his gizzard for him with his knife," he explained. "How do you like that? And with the big fool holding a gun on him. Oh, you don't monkey with Doc Sprigge, gentlemen."

Blood began to spread over the floor.

"Somebody get a doctor," yelled one of the men. "For God's sake, get a doctor."

"I'm a doctor," said Doc, calmly. "But he don't need me now. He needs an undertaker."

Frenchy shifted his legs and began to roll a cigarette. Pinto sat motionless in the lookout's chair, calmly scratching himself as if nothing at all had happened, nothing at all.

Word had spread all over the place by now, and men and girls came crowding in from the bar. One of the girls let out a hair-raising shriek at the sight of the crumpled man lying in a pool of blood, and was led out. The other girls, white-faced, merely stared. Old Dr. Ortega had been found in the bar and, showing a bewildered face, not having the faintest idea what it was all about, he allowed a group of shouting and gesticulating men to propel him into the gambling room. At the sight of the body on the floor, he stopped dead, glanced over at Doc, hesitated, then stooped down for a moment.

He rose, shaking his head. "I can't help this man. He's dead. Has Marshal Gann been notified?"

No one seemed to know. Dr. Ortega looked all about him. "Who did this?"

"I did," said Doc.

Now Mule Casper jumped in. "And I saw it all. This fool was holding a gun on Doc, threatening to shoot him. Clear case of self-defense."

There were murmurs of agreement on all sides. Dr. Ortega ran his eyes over the faces in the crowd, then he turned to Doc. "I'm acting coroner in San Ygnacio in case you don't know, Doc. Any statement you'd like to make?"

"The operation was successful," said Doc, "but the patient died."

Mule Casper guffawed and slapped his thigh. Pinto snickered in the background. But there was no general laugh; far from it; many of the men were disgusted by Doc's callousness, though afraid to say so.

"You have an odd attitude for a man of your profession," said old Dr. Ortega.

Doc merely looked at him with a bored expression. Frenchy began to hum to himself, but broke off abruptly. Now a couple of men belatedly brought a blanket and carefully covered the body.

"The marshal must be notified," said Dr. Ortega, and turning, he pushed his way through the crowd and disappeared.

"What do we do, Doc?" asked Pinto.

"We deal, if anybody's interested," said Doc.

Of those connected with the enforcement of law in San Ygnacio, Rufe Caton, one of the judge's new "clerks," was the first to hear about it. He had bumped into Juan Alvarez in Howard Street. Juan was part-owner of the feed and grain store on the corner across from the marshal's house. He seemed very excited and Rufe stopped to talk with him.

Stammering slightly, showing a shocked pale face, Juan explained what had happened.

"Did you see it?" asked Rufe.

"Yes," said Juan, "and I wish I hadn't. Doc opened him up like a sack of grain. Cut his belt clear through. His pants fell down. It was like an act in a circus. Then *he* fell down. But, Rufe—this man asked for it."

"Self-defense, eh?"

"Yes," said Juan. "As little as I think of Doc Sprigge, I'd have to say so. And there are plenty others. Joe Ballard was there. Mule Casper. Oh, a lot of the old citizens."

"Thanks, Juan," said Rufe. "I'd better see the judge."

He took off at a run along Howard Street. He'd have to work fast. Marshal Gann might put his foot in it, not knowing the facts.

He finally found the judge at the marshal's house. Although it was pretty late, the judge and Berta were still visiting together. No one else was there.

"What is it, Rufe?" asked the judge.

"Howdy, Miss Berta," said Rufe, taking off his hat; then: "I'd like to speak to you outside, Judge."

The judge excused himself and stepped out onto the stoop with Rufe, who, in a low, eager voice, explained what had happened and all the attendant circumstances.

"You're right," said the judge. "We've got to find Ben."

But when they found him he was already on his way to the Palace, trailed by Luis and Homer. The marshal had been in Mextown settling a little problem which Luis had felt that he himself couldn't handle. And the judge was grateful to whatever it was that had kept Ben off Howard Street at that precise moment. He would have gone charging in, no doubt about it, and Doc would have made a public monkey of him, with all his witnesses.

Even as it was, Ben was adamant about arresting him.

"But, Ben, there's no case," the judge pleaded. "The man had already drawn. He was standing up. Doc was sitting down. Maybe fifty witnesses, Ben, some of them old friends of 'yours. Look, Ben. Justice is justice."

"I'm going to arrest him," said Ben. "Take him to jail. I may have to release him. But he's not going to kill a man in San Ygnacio while I'm marshal and not suffer some inconvenience."

"All right," said the judge. "All right. Jail him. Then we'll have a hearing in my court."

"Tonight?"

"Yes," said the judge. "You want some shyster pestering me for a writ? I'd have to give it to him."

"All right," said Ben.

Len Cline, the judge's other "clerk," had now joined the group. Ben looked them all over sardonically.

67

"This is beginning to seem like an army," he said. "All you men stay outside. I'll make the arrest."

Young Rufe was going to protest, but the judge silenced him with a look.

"Hello, Ben," said Doc, glancing up from his dealing. "What delayed you?"

The players backed off to give the marshal plenty of room.

"Where's the body?" asked Ben.

"They moved it," said Doc. "Some place in the back."

Now Ben saw the huge blackish spot on the carpet and compressed his thin lips.

"Get your hat, Doc," he said. "You're under arrest."

Doc stood up and turned the box over. "See all of you gentlemen later." Then he turned to Ben. "Sure you want to arrest me, Ben?"

"You heard what I said."

"He drew on me. I've got plenty of witnesses. Look at the bullet hole in this table. Didn't miss my knees by two inches."

"Come on, Doc."

Doc shrugged. "Well, since it's you, Ben, an old friend . . ."

He started away, but Pinto called to him: "What do we do, Doc?"

"Wait," said Doc. "I'll be back."

Doc took his hat down from a peg on the wall and as they started out into the bar he tried to walk beside the marshal as if they were two friends just strolling around. But Ben wouldn't have it that way.

"Keep in front of me, Doc," he said. "And let's not have any trouble."

Doc chuckled. "Trouble? From me? But why? I haven't done anything. Hell, even in New York City a man is allowed to defend himself. And God knows this isn't New York City. You'll get no trouble from me, Ben."

All the same, Ben kept Doc in front of him and they crossed the long bar and went out the door in silence. A crowd was milling about in front of the Palace, as word had got around that Ben Gann had gone in to arrest Doc Sprigge for a killing. Men stared bug-eyed as the spruce little doctor appeared, followed by the old, shabby-looking marshal.

Staff was on the edge of the crowd, with his hat pulled down over his eyes. A man nudged him and he turned. "Was talking with Mule Casper," the man said. "Plain self-defense, open and shut."

"Yep," says Staff, "looks like it."

"What do you mean—looks like it?"

"Doc seldom holds still for an arrest unless he's certain he's got all the cards—so I hear."

"Why do you reckon the marshal's arresting him then?"

Staff merely shook his head. But he knew why. The marshal was out to pester Doc in as many ways as possible. Doc would probably weather this one, all right, but there'd be real trouble yet. Staff sighed and started off toward the livery barn. Old Mr. Urbey didn't get around very good any more, too much weight on his old feet—Lord, he was a fat man!—and he liked to have Staff nose around and bring him the news. Well, they'd certainly have something to talk about tonight.

Doc looked about him with distaste. The old adobe jail had a strong, musty-damp smell that no amount of disinfectant could counteract.

"You need a new jail," said Doc.

"It'll hold you," said Ben; then he held out his hand. "Gun."

Doc hesitated, then took the gun from the shoulder-holster and handed it to the marshal, who put it on the desk.

"Knife."

Doc gave up his knife with a grimace. It was in the sheath and had been carefully washed and cleansed.

Now the marshal turned to Homer. "Lock him up. Front cell."

"Wait a minute," said Doc. "I didn't hear anything about being locked up. What about the hearing?"

"As soon as the judge is ready," said the marshal. "May be tonight. May be tomorrow. Lock him up, Homer."

"Ben," said Doc.

And the marshal turned. "Yes?"

"You figure on running for governor?"

"No. Why?"

"Oh, I just wondered. Grandstanding like this. I guess I was wrong about you. I always thought you were a strong man for justice. But you're kicking me around."

"Oh, I wouldn't say that, Doc," said the marshal, indifferently. "All right, Homer."

Seething, Doc was locked into cell one. The smell was even worse in the cells. Taking out his handkerchief, Doc held it to his nose and began to pace.

The marshal sat at his desk and lit a cigar. Luis and Homer stood looking at him with pride. It took guts, real guts, to treat Doc Sprigge like this. Now Ben noticed them.

"What are you boys gawking at?" he demanded. "Get uptown. It's still Saturday night."

They went out hurriedly. Silence, like a pall, settled down over the old jail. The marshal could hear Doc pacing, and smiled to himself. Finally Doc called to him.

"Yes?" said the marshal.

"We alone, Ben?"

"We're alone."

"You'll pay for this, Ben. Just remember what I'm saying. You'll pay for this."

"Is that a threat?"

"No, Ben. Just the plain truth, that's all."

"I've heard a lot of that kind of talk from men like you in thirty years. And where are they now?"

"I've had my say," said Doc, then he began to pace again.

The hearing was held a few minutes after two a.m. in Judge Howard's little courtroom. Doc was not represented by counsel, but he had plenty of witnesses, some of them reluctant to testify on his behalf, others eager. One of the latter was Mule Casper, a real old-timer. They couldn't shut him up.

"I don't know what the West is coming to and I don't know what an old-timer like Ben Gann is thinking about to drag Doc in here. For what? For nothing! If a man pulls a gun on me I'm going to shoot him if I can. Should I be arrested for it? It's all a lot of goldarn Eastern nonsense. If it was some new young fool of a peace officer, who didn't know his business, maybe I could understand it, but . . ."

Judge Howard's gavel finally drowned him out. "Just a minute, Mule. You're not in here to make speeches. And you've given us your testimony. Stand aside."

Homer was forced to eject Mule from the courtroom, and old Mule stood by himself on the wooden sidewalk outside, still talking, and looking off at the lights of upper Howard Street.

Joe Ballard, the gunsmith, was an entirely different type of witness. He hated and feared men like Doc. And yet his testimony corroborated Mule's, and Doc's, in every respect. "I don't see what else Doc could have done," he concluded.

Other men stood about waiting to testify, studying Doc surreptitiously. Doc merely seemed irritable to them, fidgeting with his tie, but actually he was suffering an unsettling reaction that often attacked him after a fight and a killing: a feeling of unreality as if the world about him had suddenly changed and he wasn't exactly sure where he was; and this feeling was usually followed by a bleak depression, a sort of black hopelessness, which Doc always managed successfully to counteract with whisky. So Doc stood there, pulling at his tie, and wondering how long it would be until he could get himself a drink.

Now the judge was speaking. "I don't think any more testimony will be necessary. Do you, Marshal?"

Ben merely shrugged as if to say, That's up to you.

"It is most certainly a plain case of self-defense," Judge Howard went on. "There isn't a shred of dissenting testimony. Therefore, I find that there is no reason whatever for considering an indictment—of any degree—and so"— he hit the desk smartly with his gavel—"the hearing is over, and I declare that Arthur Sprigge is a free agent and shall be released without onus of any kind. Dismissed!"

Mule Casper had come back in and he hurried over and shook Doc's hand. "You're about the only one of the real boys left, Doc," he said. "All the rest are dead or buffaloed. The West's getting so it's just for women and kids—and sheepherders. Night, Doc."

Doc nodded absent-mindedly.

"Come get your belongings," said Ben, touching his arm.

"I'll send down for 'em," said Doc, in a surly voice. "No more of that stink for me."

He started off, but Ben restrained him. Doc showed violent anger, then suppressed it.

"This is not my way, Doc," said Ben. "I'm forced to listen to the judge. Left to myself, I'd have run you out of town for this. Next time I will, judge or no judge."

Doc laughed scornfully, pulled away, and went out without another word.

Someone put a hand on Ben's arm and he turned.

It was the judge. "You don't look happy, Ben," he said.

"How could I be?" snapped Ben. "He's free, isn't he?"

The judge shrugged and sighed.

Staff woke with a start and lit a match to look at Pop's watch on the near-by desk. Nearly three-thirty. He'd heard footsteps outside the office door, which was kept open.

"Who is it?" he called, sitting up.

"It's me—Doc Sprigge. Is that you, Stafford? Hell, I didn't know you lived here."

Astonished, Staff got up and lit a lantern. Doc was standing in the doorway.

"What do you want, Doc?"

"I want to rent a horse."

Staff studied him. "You mean you want to *buy* one, don't you?"

Doc laughed. "You think they run me out? Don't be foolish. I just want a horse for an hour or two. I want to ride out in the open country and get a certain smell out of my nose. Maybe I want to communicate with my Maker under the Eternal Stars." Doc was speaking with elaborate sarcasm now.

Staff kept looking at him. The little man was in an odd state of mind of some kind. Now Doc moved a little farther into the office and Staff caught a strong smell of whisky. Drunk, that was it. As drunk as Doc ever got, that is. Dangerous and all his wits about him, drunk or sober.

"The thing is," said Doc, "there's nobody for me to talk to any more, so sometimes I ride out and talk to the mountains. Nobody talks my language now—except maybe an occasional old fool like Mule Casper. It's all gone, fellow, all gone. And Doc's still here. And that's the trouble."

"I'll see that you get a horse, Doc," said Staff.

"You could talk to me, fellow," said Doc. "I know that. But you won't."

"I'll get Pete," said Staff. "We'll fix you up."

Staff left hurriedly. Doc leaned against the doorjamb and stared as if fascinated at the lantern.

"That's the trouble," he said. "Nobody to talk to."

VI

It was another bright and sunny spring day. Berta, finished
with her housework for the morning, changed her dress,
freshened herself up, then decided that she'd take a walk up
to Boggs's general store—not that she needed anything—
the larder was full—but she just couldn't face the prospect
of sitting around the house on such a day. And then perhaps
she might—she just might—happen to run into Staff, but
she kept this thought at the back of her mind.

The sky was cloudless and pale blue, the air thin and dry.
The mountains looked so close that it was almost as if they
had crept in on the town during the night. Up ahead of
Berta, as she emerged from the house, Howard Street
seemed to be sleeping in the blaze of the day. On the shady
side, saddled horses drowsed at the hitchracks, occasionally
stomping and switching flies.

"What a day for a ride," she thought, and then she began
to wonder if Mrs. Graham would like to take a little jaunt
with her out to Ferguson's ranch, which was only a few
miles from town.

Mrs. Graham was a cheerful widow of forty-three, or so
she said. She lived on Indian Road with her sister and her
brother-in-law, Colonel Drayer. The colonel, an old man
with long white hair and a white mustache and imperial,
was not a colonel at all, but a former army scout, now
retired and living on a pension. He was, Ben Gann said, the

biggest and most amusing liar in San Ygnacio. If you listened to him closely you came away with the impression that he had defeated the Mescalero Apaches single-handed. But no one, except for laughs, ever listened to him closely any more.

Mrs. Graham was Berta's only feminine confidante. They talked together endlessly about "love and men," though of course in a very nice way. Mrs. Graham had heard quite a lot about Staff from Berta and was extremely eager to make his acquaintance. She was a very unusual woman in at least one respect. Sworn to secrecy by Berta, she honored the oath. Even her own sister did not know that Berta was in the "throes of a love affair," as Mrs. Graham put it to herself. Also she was secretive about her opinion of Ben Gann. She did not like him at all; she felt all thumbs and girlish around him; and seldom came near the Gann house unless she was sure he was absent. "He makes me feel like a fool or something," she admitted to herself. "Doesn't appreciate Berta. Makes a slavey out of her. Men can be so trying!"

Preoccupied with thoughts of Mrs. Graham and of a slow pleasant ride out to Ferguson's ranch, Berta came to herself suddenly when a rider emerged from an alley across the street, leading three horses. Staff! It couldn't be. But it was.

He saw her at once and took off his hat. She smiled and waved. Now he turned south on Howard Street. Berta held her breath. Was it possible that he was taking the horses out to Ferguson's? Old Mr. Ferguson had a lot of horse-dealing with Mr. Urbey. But, no; that would be too— It was almost like telepathy, a little frightening!

And then she noticed that Staff wasn't going to stop and talk to her! She hesitated, looked about her, then hurried down the old warped wooden sidewalk under the wooden awning, and intercepted him at the next alleyway.

He seemed uncomfortable as he pulled up and took his hat off again.

"Hello," she said, laughing nervously.

"Morning, Miss Berta."

"Where are you taking those horses?" she asked.

"Out to Ferguson's," said Staff. "Came in and picked them out last night, the old man did."

"Oh, out to Ferguson's," said Berta, not knowing what else to say.

"Yes," said Staff, "and I'd better be on my way. Mr. Urbey worries when I'm not at the barn. Mighty nice seeing you, Miss Berta."

Staff nodded, smiled, then rode on. Berta stood looking after him, then, trying not to hurry, she started back down Howard Street and when she reached the end of it, she crossed Indian Road and knocked at Colonel Drayer's door. It was opened immediately and Mrs. Graham stood smiling at her.

"I saw you coming, dear," she said. "And I saw *him*. He just rode past, leading three horses. My, he's thin! Come in. Come in."

"No," said Berta. "I won't come in. But I was wondering, since it's such a nice day and all, if you'd like to take a ride out to Ferguson's."

Mrs. Graham's eyes showed amusement, then she laughed. "Why, of course, dear. Of course."

"Fine," cried Berta, flushed and flustered. "Homer's at the jail. I'll send him up for the horses and we can start right away. All right?"

"Yes," said Mrs. Graham. "You're a godsend, dear. I've been racking my brain for an excuse to get out of this house. The colonel"—she looked over her shoulder hastily—"well, he's got one of his talking spells, and I'm really fed up with the Apache Wars."

But there were unforeseen delays. Homer was *not* at the jail. He'd been called away. And Ben had warned Berta not to go up to the corral after the horses any more. Everybody seemed to have disappeared. Berta fumed and fretted. It was nearly half an hour before she ran down Rufe Caton and sent him to the corral.

But now at last she and Mrs. Graham were far out of town, on their way to Ferguson's ranch. Berta was still flushed and irritated. "Sometimes men drive me crazy," she said.

"Yes," said Mrs. Graham, in her comfortable voice, "they can be such fools—so thick-headed. I often wonder if they do it on purpose."

"That Rufe!" said Berta. "I don't know what he was doing at the corral. He would have had time to ride out to the spur and back. And I told him to hurry. He knew I was furious. He kept apologizing."

"Oh, well," said Mrs. Graham, soothingly, "no harm done. We're on our way and it's a beautiful day. Listen to the birds singing in the bushes."

Now they rode in silence at an easy gait. Berta was wearing her jeans, the seat of which she had secretly let out, working when Ben wasn't around; Mrs. Graham had on a divided, buckskin skirt. "It makes me look like a balloon about to rise," she had once told Berta, "but at my age I simply can't wear jeans. Sis tried it, you know, and the colonel told her her rear looked like a sack of potatoes."

A dusty, narrow old road, hardly more than a trail, wound off to the west, past tall rocks and huge cottonwood trees, toward the Ferguson ranch, which nestled in among low, barren hills in the higher tableland. The heavy rains of spring had brightened all of the vegetation, the grass was tall beyond the road, and there were riotous lush patches of wild flowers here and there, red, pale blue, golden yellow.

"Oh, aren't they beautiful!" cried Mrs. Graham. "Look over there, Berta. A field of gold. I've never seen so many wild flowers as this spring."

"Yes," said Berta, absent-mindedly.

After a pause, Mrs. Graham asked: "How is our little affair progressing?"

"I'm afraid it's not progressing at all. I think he's too modest," said Berta. "That's the only explanation I can think of. I know he likes me. I know it."

"Of course he does. How could he help it?"

Berta sighed. "But it's so complicated, with Ben interfering and all. I just don't know."

"Fathers are always interfering. It's partly jealously," said Mrs. Graham. "Mine did."

"And you married anyway?" asked Berta, turning to look at Mrs. Graham.

"I certainly did. And then it was all right. My father quieted down."

Suddenly, beyond the rocks up ahead, shots were fired. Berta's horse threw up its head and nickered nervously.

"What's that?" asked Berta. "Who would be shooting out here?"

The firing continued, then they heard loud yells and laughing.

"Oh, well," said Mrs. Graham, "whoever it is, they seem to be having a good time."

They rode on. More firing, more yells and laughing, and then a sudden stillness—an almost frightening stillness. Berta and Mrs. Graham glanced at each other uneasily. And then at a turn in the road, as it wound round a huge, grotesquely eroded rock, they gasped and pulled up abruptly. Two men were standing in the middle of the road, blocking it. One was tall and black-bearded; the other was red-headed and freckle-faced. They were strangers, outlanders, both wearing filthy old trail clothes and two guns apiece.

"Don't be alarmed, ladies," said the bearded one. "We're just having a little target practice. We're heading for San Ygnacio and figure we might need it."

"We're not alarmed," said Berta, and tried to urge her horse forward, but the men blocked her way, grinning.

"Would you ladies like to get down and see us shoot?" asked the red-headed one. "We're pretty good."

"No, thank you," said Mrs. Graham.

"Why, don't thank me, lady," said the black-bearded one. "You ain't got anything to thank me for—yet." The

78

red-headed one guffawed and slapped his thigh. "Hey, look," the black-bearded one went on, "there's your twin. Look at that carrot-colored hair."

"Yes, sir," said the red-headed one, grinning. "She's sure got real red hair. Ain't many of us, miss. We're the exception in this here world."

"Stand aside," said Berta. "We're going on."

The men hesitated and glanced at each other, but they made no move to get out of the way.

"Why don't you ladies be sociable?" asked the black-bearded one. "We been on the trail for some time and we sure would appreciate a little relaxation."

His words seemed to incite the red-headed one, who now jumped forward and grabbed Mrs. Graham's bridle. She suppressed a scream, then fumbled futilely with her riding crop.

Suddenly the men paused and looked off. They'd heard something. In a moment a horseman came round the edge of the big rock. He had one leg over the pommel of his saddle and he was rolling a cigarette. Staff!

The red-headed one let go of the bridle and moved back. "Now where in hell did he come from?"

"Just some fool cowpoke," said the black-bearded one. "Ain't even heeled."

Without a word, Staff rode up and joined the group. "Hello, Miss Berta," he said.

"This is Mrs. Graham," said Berta, controlling her voice with difficulty. "Mr. Stafford."

Mrs. Graham's face was white and she spoke through stiff lips. "How do you do?"

Staff appeared to notice nothing out of the way.

"Well, now I never!" said the black-bearded one. "A tea party! You figure to just ride on, fellow?"

"Yeah," said Staff, mildly. "I figure to ride on. But coming in across the flat over there I saw you fellows shooting at cans. You're not very good, are you?"

The two men looked at each other in astonishment, then

laughed. "Why, you dumb cow-rassler," said the black-bearded one, "if you knew who we were!"

"I used to do a little shooting—for money," said Staff. "Bet you three to one—thirty to ten—I can do something with a six-shooter you can't do."

"Aw, you're crazy."

Red-head leaned over and whispered to his pal. "Maybe trying to get his hands on a gun."

"What good would that do him?" asked the black-bearded one, and they both laughed. Then he turned to Staff. "I don't shoot for peanuts, mister. Git up some real money or git."

"I got three hundred dollars."

"Now you're talking. Three hundred to a hundred. Right?"

"Okay," said Staff, swinging down from his horse. "Give me a gun."

"You back off, Red," said the black-bearded one, "and be ready just in case."

Red backed off to the other side of the road and kept his hands near his guns. The black-bearded one tossed Staff a gun. Staff caught it deftly.

"Now throw your money down," called blackbeard.

Staff reached into his shirt pocket and got out a roll of bills with a band round it and tossed it on the ground.

"Okay, ante," said Staff.

Blackbeard grimaced, then grudgingly threw a couple of bills on the ground. "I'll just have to pick 'em up again," he grumbled.

"Ready?" called Staff.

"Okay. Ready."

Staff stepped back, took off his hat and sailed it up high in the air. Raising the gun, he fired three quick shots. The hat jumped slightly, then fell to the ground.

"Thought I'd ventilate the brim a little," said Staff. "Pick it up. Look at it."

Blackbeard retrieved the hat and stood staring at it, with

his big mouth open. There were three perforations in the brim, about an inch apart and in a straight line, as if punched by a machine. Blackbeard was staggered. Without a word he held the hat up and showed it to Red. Then he turned and studied Staff. There was a shadow of fear, of panic even, in his dark eyes.

"Who are you, mister?" he asked.

"Go ahead. Shoot," said Staff. "Take your turn."

Blackbeard dropped Staff's hat, then he took off his own and scratched his head. "Mister," he said, "you got my pet gun."

Staff laughed at him. Blackbeard looked over at Red in bewilderment, then he turned back to Staff and said: "No. No use me shooting. Hell, nobody can shoot that good. It's impossible."

"All right then," said Staff. "Pick up your money and *git!*" He yelled the "git" and his voice had the sting of a whiplash.

Berta looked at him in amazement, her face pale, her lips parted. Then she turned to glance at Mrs. Graham, but Mrs. Graham was staring at Staff as if fascinated.

"You won it," said Blackbeard, weakly.

"Take it and *git!*"

Blackbeard picked up his money, looked about him vaguely as if he weren't quite sure whether this was a dream or what, then he and Red swung into their saddles and rode off down the trail, toward San Ygnacio.

Staff picked up his hat and put it on and restored Mr. Urbey's roll of bills to his pocket. It seemed that he couldn't bring himself to look at Berta and Mrs. Graham.

"Staff! Staff!" cried Berta, and he turned swiftly. "She's going to faint. She's going to faint."

Staff ran over to Mrs. Graham and held her up in her saddle.

"Let's get out in the open," he said. "Away from these rocks where I can watch those fellows."

Leading his own horse and propping Mrs. Graham up,

Staff moved around the big rock and into a wide flat open space, shaded by a large cottonwood tree. Berta followed on her horse, riding up as close to him as possible. She still felt terrified. He glanced up at her.

"Well, Miss Berta," he said, "I guess you've got a pretty good idea what kind of fellow I am now."

Staff had made Mrs. Graham comfortable in the shade of the cottonwood tree. She was lying on a blanket with her saddle for a pillow. She looked pale and shaken.

"Feeling better?" asked Berta.

"Yes," said Mrs. Graham. "But what would we have done if he hadn't come along? Those horrible men!"

And suddenly Berta remembered what Ben had told her about the "wolves" gathering for the kill.

"Well, he did," she said, soothingly. "So let's not worry about that any more."

Mrs. Graham turned her head on the saddle. "Where is he?"

Berta pointed. "He's right over there on a little rise, watching those men. He says if they show any signs of coming back we'll start for Ferguson's. But they won't," Berta added, a proud note in her voice.

"No," said Mrs. Graham, "I don't think they will either. They seemed scared to death to me."

"I—I just don't know what to say," said Berta. "It's as if I didn't know him. But then, come to think of it, one time when I was talking to him at the livery barn a little man came in that Staff didn't like, and you should have seen his eyes. Mrs. Graham, I just don't know what to think."

"Well," said Mrs. Graham, "all I can say is, he's a mighty nervy man, and slick. If he'd 've ridden in and started making a row they might have shot him. But, no, he outfoxed them. I see what you mean, Berta. Takes practice."

"Yes," said Berta, but for reasons so obscure that she

wasn't sure of them herself, she didn't repeat to Mrs. Graham what Staff had said to her as they were riding round the big rock: "I guess you've got a pretty good idea what kind of a fellow I am now."

She heard footsteps and turned. Staff had come down off the rise and was walking toward her, dangling the big, long-barreled .45 in his right hand.

"Are they gone?"

Staff nodded. "Yeah. Never even looked back. The trail's downhill from here. I could see them for a long ways and then when I couldn't see them any longer I could see their dust. How's the lady?"

"She's feeling better. But I think we should let her rest for a while."

"Yes. Must have been quite a shock for a nice lady like that—and for you too, Miss Berta. But after all, you're just a young girl and that makes a big difference."

"I'm not so young," said Berta, rather indignantly. "I'm nineteen."

Staff glanced at her and smiled. "As old as all that?"

He looked so kind now, so boyish, so sympathetic. Berta's mind was in confusion. She didn't know what she thought. But she knew what she felt. As far as she was concerned there was just nobody in the world but Staff. She could feel herself flushing, and hastily lowered her eyes.

Staff noticed her confusion, without being aware of the reason for it, and turning he walked over to the horses and slipped the gun into the saddle-bag on Berta's saddle.

"Don't you want it?" asked Berta.

"No," said Staff. "Get Mr. Gann to load it for you—two shots still left in it—and take it with you after this when you ride out in the country."

"Oh, I couldn't shoot anybody."

"Wouldn't have helped you much with those fellows, that's a fact," said Staff. "But they're exceptional."

"What do you mean?"

"Real cowardly bad ones; knife-in-the-back types. Your

father knows all about those kind. And they'll be coming into San Ygnacio from all directions now. Maybe you better just not go riding at all, Miss Berta, unless you take Homer or somebody along."

Berta glanced at him with a questioning, an almost pleading, look in her eyes, but he kept his own eyes lowered and began to roll a cigarette. She watched him in silence for a moment, then she turned to look at Mrs. Graham.

"She's got her eyes closed," she whispered to Staff. "I think she's dozing."

"Well," said Staff, "I ought to be getting back on account of Mr. Urbey—but—I guess he won't mind too much. Wonderful man. Like a father to me."

Berta hesitated, then sat down with her back to the trunk of the cottonwood tree. Staff lit his cigarette, shifted about for a moment, then sat down near her.

"You think she can hear us?" he asked, after a long pause.

Berta glanced at him in surprise. "No. I don't think so."

After another long pause Staff said: "For quite a while now I've wanted to have a talk with you, Miss Berta."

She glanced at him eagerly, then lowered her eyes. "You have? Why?"

"Well, first off," said Staff, "every time we meet I kind of run away. Have you noticed that?"

"Yes."

Staff smiled slightly. "Well, one night your father took the trouble to have a little confab with me. He told me he didn't want me talking to you like I'd been—and I told him he was right."

"Oh, I didn't know this," said Berta, flushing uncomfortably. "He didn't tell me. And why is he right?"

"I'm coming to that," said Staff. "Miss Berta, I've been in some kind of trouble since I was seventeen years old. I been through six range wars. I had a dozen warrants out for me till the Governor declared that amnesty. Now I'm not wanted any more. But that's beside the point."

Berta couldn't bring herself to speak. She just sat there looking at him.

"Yes, ma'am," he went on. "I'm twenty-eight years old and I've been on the run, you might say, the last eleven of 'em."

Berta broke in. "But you're not on the run now!"

"Only from myself," said Staff.

There was a pause. Staff had smoked his cigarette down until it was almost burning his lips. He tossed it away and began to roll another one.

"I'd like to tell you about it if you don't mind."

"Oh, please do," said Berta, rather awkwardly, feeling nervous, unsure.

"Well," said Staff, lighting the fresh cigarette, "I won't go into detail—no use in that. Anyway, none of it would mean much to you. So I'll just say this. I was in the middle of a range war. A bunch of us had been hired to protect about a dozen ranches. The peace officers just wouldn't do anything, you understand? And anyway there wasn't enough of them. A bad bunch of boys from the Nations— some of them breeds and even full-blooded Comanches— had been hoorahing the ranches, shooting at the hands, running off the stock, especially horseflesh, and doing a fine business with the stolen stock with blackleg ranchers back in the hills. Well, we tangled with the gang in an arroyo and there was a big fight. We surprised them and we really gave them a bad time. They got away finally. But I'll bet you there wasn't one sound man in the outfit. We really peppered them." He paused and glanced at the smoke rising from his cigarette. "Am I too long-winded, Miss Berta?"

"No," said Berta. "Not at all. Please go on."

"Now there's something I want you to understand, in all fairness. I say we were protecting the ranchers. Sounds nice, but the law didn't see it that way. The law couldn't see any difference between us and the gang from the Nations. We weren't officers; we had no badges and no authority. Well, things got pretty bad—a lot of killing. So the Governor just outlawed everybody on both sides. It didn't help—didn't faze the ranchers; all they worried about was their livestock. So the fighting went on, got worse. Thirty men were killed in one week, in and around the little town that was in the middle of all this.''

"Thirty men!" cried Berta, appalled.

"Yeah," said Staff. "That's pretty bad. Well, there were four of us who always stuck together. Roy, Frank, Tucson, and me. We rode with the big mobs and all that, but when the range shooting would simmer down a little, we'd take off and camp together. Roy was my especial friend; we were the same age, liked the same things, had a lot of fun together. I was going to say he was like a brother; but he was closer than that. I never got along too well with my real brothers. Well, finally one night the four of us—this was a year ago, this spring—the four of us, we made a big town at the north of the range. There was some kind of official celebration going on and the town was packed. There'd been some shooting earlier, so the marshal had deputized a hundred citizens and they were patrolling the streets and the bars. When you went into a bar on this night they made you check your guns. No man was allowed to wear guns unless he was just riding into town, or leaving. We put our horses in a public corral and went uptown to a bar. They made us check our guns at the door. Well, we'd walked into the wrong bar by pure accident. There, lined up, was almost a dozen of the gang from the Nations. But we couldn't back out. We couldn't run from them. So we just walked up to the bar and ordered.

"Well, of course the fighting starts in a few minutes. A real brannigan, with fists and chairs. It's about three to one and we are getting the worst of it, when Tucson has a bright idea. The tables in this place were very big—round and heavy. Tucson spills one of them over, then rolls it into the bunch from the Nations, knocking two or three of them down. We roll tables for a while, moving over closer to the door all the time—and pretty soon we make a break for it and get away into the street, leaving our guns behind. We had to.

"Tucson yells: 'Scatter, everybody—and meet at the corral.' So we scattered. The Nations guys had blood in their eyes by now and instead of rushing right after us, they picked up their guns, and then came out to hunt us through the town, digging up a lot more of their gang, who were hanging out in different bars.

"Well, I just couldn't see myself slinking through alleys, naked as a jaybird as far as guns were concerned, so I went into a gunsmith's and bought myself a .45, then I started for the corral. This town had kerosene street lamps and you couldn't see very good by them. And they sure made the town look dismal. Well, I'm getting along fine until I start across a certain street and there right on the corner is a bunch of the Nations guys. If I ran, they'd run after me. If I stopped and stood there they'd wonder. So I just continued on across the street except I kept angling and angling away from them. I made it. They weren't sure. They just stood there arguing. I kept going, but finally I just had to look back—and here they came; some on the sidewalk, some in the street. Quite a ways up ahead was an alley that led direct to the corral. I decided to try to make it. I slipped my gun out and carried it in my right hand. I was getting along all right until I happened to notice a lone guy, getting closer and closer, on the far side of the street. And as I was looking, he passed under one of those kerosene street lamps and I saw the glint of a gun in his hand. He had me, no doubt about that. So I just turned and shot him." Staff broke off.

Berta was staring with her mouth open. "You—you shot him?" she gasped. And then she noticed how pale Staff's face was.

He nodded. "Yes, I shot him. He fell face down in the street. Then he yelled to me once or twice, called me by name. It was Roy. He'd been trying to protect me."

Berta recoiled and stared at Staff in horror. "You mean—it was your friend—?"

"Yes," said Staff, in a choked voice. "Well—I lost my head and ran, leaving Roy there. All the Nations boys came on the run now. The only thing was they stopped to see who had been shot and when they saw it was Roy they got all mixed up and hesitated for a long time. I lit out for the corral, I grabbed a horse without any saddle, any old horse, and got away. . . ."

"Staff," cried Berta, "you're going too fast for me. Wait. Why did you shoot Roy?"

"I thought he was one of the Nations gang. I thought he'd outfigured me. I was too quick on the trigger, that's all. *I was too quick!* That's the trouble with guns."

"Oh, Staff," said Berta, tears in her eyes, "I'm so sorry." She didn't know what to say. She felt totally inadequate.

Staff rolled another cigarette and sat nodding to himself. "Yes," he said. "It's pretty hard to imagine anything worse happening. Well, I hid out in a little Mexican village till the next night, then I borrowed a saddle, a rifle, and another gun and went back. But the celebration was over and the town was almost deserted. The Nations boys had lit out, due to the shooting of Roy, who died almost right away, so I heard. So I got a room at a hotel and stayed around for the funeral. I put a wreath on his grave, and I swore an oath I'd never wear guns again."

There was a long silence. One of the horses stomped, and switched at the flies. Mrs. Graham turned restlessly on her blanket, sighed heavily, then settled down again.

"But—but, Staff, it was an accident," said Berta, muddled, uncertain, feeling at a loss.

"Yes," said Staff. "But that don't change anything. Miss Berta, I guess I haven't made myself plain. During the range wars I was what they call a badman. I got started wrong at seventeen; a lot of the boys did, but that's no excuse. I kept on till I shot Roy. I was a damned pig-headed fool, if you'll excuse the language. So you see, the marshal's right. You listen to him, Miss Berta. He's got your best interests at heart."

Berta felt like crying. She sat looking at Staff, who was staring at the ground and idly tossing a pebble from one hand to the other. "You listen to him," he repeated, as if to himself.

Staff rode with them to the edge of town where he pulled up.

"I don't think we ought to say anything about this, ladies, do you?" he asked, smiling.

"No," said Berta. "I don't think we should. Ben would have a fit. Is that all right with you, Mrs. Graham?"

"Perfectly all right."

Staff gestured and started off. "I'll take a back way," he said. "You're okay now."

They watched him go, then they rode off toward Howard Street and home.

"It just seems like a nightmare now," said Mrs. Graham. "I'm going up to my room and soak my feet and go to bed. No supper for me." Now she turned and looked at Berta, who was pale and seemed withdrawn. "You had quite a talk," she went on. "I dozed and dozed. Every time I opened my eyes you were talking."

"I'll—I'll tell you all about it later," said Berta, hastily, "after I've thought it over."

"Well, for God's sake, Staff," Pop was saying, "I thought maybe the Injuns had got you."

"Here's the money, Mr. Urbey," said Staff, hastily putting the roll on the desk. "Now do you mind if I go uptown for a little while? There's something I've got to take care of."

Pop looked at him in surprise, but said: "No, son, no. You sick? You look kinda pale, Staff."

"No, I'm fine, and I'll be back just as soon as I can get here."

He left abruptly. Pop sat staring after him, wondering, worried. He didn't know what he'd do without the boy.

Staff hurried in and out of saloon after saloon. Finally he found Blackbeard and Red at the little Las Vegas Bar, just behind the Long Horn Hotel. They started at the sight of him and Red drew back as if to run. Staff pushed them ahead of him to the end of the bar where there were no eavesdroppers.

"Now listen," he said. "No talk about my shooting, understand? I live in this town. I work here. I don't want any such talk floating around."

The glitter of his gray eyes, the pale grim face scared them.

"No, hell, no," stammered Red.

"We don't know you from Adam," said Blackbeard, solemnly.

"And don't forget it," said Staff. "If I hear any talk I'll know where it came from."

He turned and went out. Red whistled, pushed his hat back, and taking out a bandanna, mopped his forehead.

"I wish I knew who he was," said Blackbeard. "He must be hiding out."

"Yeah," said Red. "Must be."

"Say," said Blackbeard, "I understand Doc Sprigge's in town. You figure he could shoot like that?"

"Nobody can shoot like that," said Red. "It must have been an accident."

"He called the turn. He called the turn," cried Blackbeard, slapping the bar.

Red groaned and went on mopping his forehead.

VII

Old Mule Casper tore out of the stage station and hurried across the intersection of Howard and San Juan to his favorite post in front of the Long Horn Hotel. He was shaking with excitement and he kept looking about him eagerly for somebody to talk to. But men passed him, one after another, and not a familiar face! God, how the town was growing and filling up with strangers from Lord knows where. Mule shrugged in annoyance, then took out his plug of tobacco and bit off a huge chew. Just as he was putting it away his eyes lit up and he turned quickly toward a man who had just come out of the hotel.

"Doc," he called. "Doc."

It was a little early in the day for Doc to be out. He'd slept poorly the night before and he felt surly and irritable. He merely glanced at Mule and then started on across the street. Mule caught up with him and walked beside him.

"Doc," he said, "you know Jim Trahan, don't you?"

Doc exploded. "Know him! Why, that big, loud-mouthed—!" Suddenly he broke off and turned to look at Mule. "Why?"

"Well," said Mule, delighted to be the first to give Doc the information, "he just got in on the Apache Rock stage. Got that Gila Sam fellow with him."

They had crossed the street now and Doc stopped on the

corner, took out a stogie, and lit up, then turned his full attention to Mule. Men passed endlessly, many of them looking at Doc and nudging their companions. Mule gazed about him proudly. There he was, old Mule Casper, burro-wrangler and desert rat, hobnobbing with the West's number-one man, Doc Sprigge.

"I talked to 'em," Mule was saying. "You see, I guided Jim and a party through the Mogollons once. At the time he was sure in one hell of a hurry to get to New Mexico, but I don't know why. I don't ask questions."

"He'd probably just shot somebody in the back," snapped Doc.

Mule stared. "Oh, I was figuring he was quite a gunfighter, Doc. Gila Sam is, ain't he?"

"Sam's great shooting at tin cans, but not so good with a man in front of him, shooting back," said Doc. "Jim Trahan's a gun-fanner, all that nonsense. Give me one clear shot. That's all I ask."

"Well, I swan," said Mule. "I thought they was pretty good."

"They're pretty good second flight," said Doc, grudgingly. "Hickok or Wyatt would have eaten them both for breakfast. What's Jim doing here? Did he say?"

"I'm coming to that," said Mule, eagerly. "He was asked in—to deal at the Nugget."

"Oh, competition," said Doc, laughing.

"Yeah," said Mule. "The Palace is killing all the other places, on account of you, I guess, Doc."

"You *guess!*" snapped Doc.

"Oh, I know," said Mule, hastily. "It was only a manner of speaking."

"Well," drawled Doc, "maybe they'll get some of the overflow."

Mule guffawed and slapped his thigh. Doc stood puffing thoughtfully on his stogie, and glancing across the street at the Nugget, a narrow bar that was jammed in between the Long Horn Hotel and McCarthy's Chicago Lunch Room. It was almost directly across Howard Street from the Palace. Now Doc's eyes lit up.

"There they are now," he said, chuckling; then he tossed his stogie away and started back across the street.

Mule, almost hugging himself with delight, followed at a respectful distance. Jim Trahan and Gila Sam were going east on San Juan and had now almost reached the entrance of the Long Horn. Sam was carrying a new rifle, so they had apparently just come from Ballard's gun store. Jim Trahan was a tall, heavy man, about thirty-five, dressed in the conventional dark clothes of the professional dealer. He was wearing two guns low on his thighs. Sam, an ex-cowhand and army scout, and about the same age, had on a short plains coat and tight pants out over his boots. He was short, bowlegged and shifty-eyed. He also was wearing two guns.

Doc was dressed in his gray suit and red tie and was not visibly armed. "Looks like an Eastern tenderfoot, except for the hat," thought Mule. "Doggone, appearances are sure deceptive."

Jim stopped in his tracks at the sight of Doc, then recovered and came on. Sam's mouth twitched nervously, and he shifted his cud of tobacco from one side to the other.

"Hi, boys," said Doc. "Well, damned if it isn't like old times. They're coming in, one by one. Jim—in case you don't know—the Nugget's just a hole-in-the-wall, not much of a place."

Jim ran his eyes over Doc, then glanced beyond him at Mule. "I see that old buzzard's been carrying the news," he said. "Well, no harm done. I'm setting up shop now, come one come all."

Doc turned his attention to Sam. "How's your marksmanship now, Sam? I understand you win all the money shooting at cans."

"Oh, I don't know," said Sam, grinning.

"How's your draw? Still slow?"

"Oh, I don't know."

Doc laughed. "Sam, with you I can never figure out whether it's modesty or stupidity."

Sam merely shifted his feet, then shifted his quid.

"Well, it's sure not modesty with you, Doc," said Jim, and Sam cackled in the background.

Doc looked at Jim with amazement. "Good God, Jim—what's happened to you? A bright remark at last."

Jim's mouth went grim. "Look, Doc. I'm not going to take any of your sass."

"Oh," said Doc, "you want to get serious, eh? Can't pass a few quips without losing your temper. Now, now, Jim."

"Come on, Sam," said Jim. "Why waste our time?"

Sam looked Doc over carefully. "Don't you go heeled no more, Doc? I like that there suit."

"He's heeled, you can bet," said Jim. "He couldn't walk down any street in the West otherwise."

"Those heavy guns takes the crease out of my pants," said Doc, insolently. "And I hate to look like a bum."

He snapped out the last word. A wave of fury passed over Jim's face, but he controlled himself and turned away, up Howard Street, toward the Nugget.

"Nice seeing you, Sam," said Doc, mildly. "How was Apache Rock?"

"We just passed through," said Sam. "Well, I'll be going."

He shifted, smiled awkwardly, then turned and followed Jim Trahan.

"A pretty pair," said Doc.

"You talked mighty rough to 'em, Doc," said Mule, delighted.

"Oh, we're pals. Banter, you know. Old man," he went on, "compared to that pretty pair I'm honest."

Mule guffawed.

"It's the truth," said Doc. "The only way to win at their table is grab the cash and run."

* * *

"Trahan and Gila Sam," Staff was saying to Pop Urbey.

"Oh, yeah," said Pop. "Jim Trahan. I've heard of him. He's a big gun, isn't he?"

"So they say," said Staff, shrugging. "Sam used to be an army scout, against the Apaches. He's seen some rough times."

"You know these fellows, Staff?"

"No. Just about them. I've been in towns where they were. I saw Jim dealing once in northern New Mexico. It was a rough place. He had a fellow sitting right beside him with a shotgun across his lap."

"Going to deal at the Nugget, eh?"

"Yeah," said Staff. "He was asked in. Trying to take the wind out of Doc's sails, I guess."

"Might be trouble," said Pop.

"Oh, I don't know," said Staff, mildly. "Ought to be room for two well-known dealers here. How about I bring you in your supper like last night?"

"Staff," said Pop, "I'm sure putting you to a lot of trouble."

"No trouble. I'll bring my own back. We'll eat together. Okay?"

Pop beamed. "Okay, son. Okay."

That night the Nugget was packed and men were standing outside trying to get in. Jim Trahan, cleanly shaved and immaculately dressed, dealt languidly, calling the cards in a weary, almost inaudible voice. Sam, in a red shirt and white silk tie, sat in the lookout's chair, while a Nugget employee, one of the bartenders, kept the cases.

A few of the old citizens came out of curiosity: Mule Casper, Joe Ballard, Juan Alvarez, and Al Tweedy from Boggs's general store. Blackbeard and Red were also bucking the box, and in a little while Staff came in, stood on

95

the edge of the crowd for a few moments, with his hat over his eyes, then turned, and went out.

"Those fellows are sure shearing the sheep," he told Pop later. "It's a massacre."

Pop chuckled over his beer.

Across the street at the Palace, Pinto was dealing. The crowd was not quite as large as usual, but you could hardly notice the difference. Men kept asking where Doc was. "Oh, he'll be back," Pinto would reply negligently.

Doc was in Sol Reed's office with Sol and Sol's lawyer, Ross Bagley. Scattered on the desk in front of them was a mass of papers. Sol's face was very pale and he kept wiping his forehead with a big white silk handkerchief. The lawyer's face was tight and grim.

"This way," said Doc, "you pay me no salary at all, not a cent. Just percentage."

"The percentage is fine, Doc," said Bagley. "We agree to that without a quibble. But the property angle is something that—"

"Oh, Sol agrees," said Doc carelessly. "That's the main thing. Right, Sol?"

Sol mopped his forehead in silence, avoiding the lawyer's eyes.

"Right, Sol?" snapped Doc.

"Yes, yes," said Sol.

"You mean you'll sign this, Sol?" asked the lawyer in distress.

"I—I haven't any alternative," said Sol.

"Why not?"

Doc slapped the table. "Never mind 'why not?'! Let him sign. I want a third, all around, property, equipment, everything. Sign, Sol."

Bagley jumped up and started out. "If you sign that, Sol," he called from the door, "I'm through as your lawyer. I'd never countenance such a thing. Why, it's highway robbery."

Furious, Doc was across the room in three bounds and

had the lawyer by the upper arms, shaking him. "Mister," he said, "you'll go back there and sit down, or you'll be a dead lawyer. That son-of-a-bitch over there tried to get me murdered in Dodge. He owes me something, see? He owes me something."

Bagley's arms went limp. Doc released him.

"Is that true, Sol?" asked the lawyer, his voice trembling slightly. "Is it true?"

Sol didn't say anything at all, but just sat with his head lowered, sweating.

The lawyer walked back to the desk and sat down. "All right, Sol," he said. "Sign it—all five copies."

Sol picked up the pen with shaking hand. Doc lit a stogie and stood looking on, smiling sardonically.

"Will wonders never cease!" he said. "Doc a property-owner. A solid citizen at last."

The lawyer ignored him, and got very busy shifting the papers for Sol's wavering signature.

At a little after eleven, warned by an odd murmur that passed around the room, Jim Trahan held up the turn of the card for a moment and raised his eyes from the table. Marshal Ben Gann was standing in front of him and the players were moving back to give him plenty of room.

"Why, hello, Ben," said Jim, smiling broadly, very friendly. "How are you? Remember Gila Sam?"

"I remember you both only too well," said Ben, who was rocking slightly on his boot-heels, his thumbs hooked in his gun-belt. "Jim! Sam! I'm telling you just what I told Doc Sprigge. You're not wanted here. I prefer you leave."

"Aw, now, Ben," said Jim, "is that any way to talk to an old-timer like me? We've hit many frontiers together, Ben. You never talked like this to me before."

"Times are changing," said Ben, "and I'm not going to just stand by and watch San Ygnacio made the last hell-town in the West. We don't want you here."

Jim sat shaking his head as if deeply aggrieved. "I don't understand it, Ben. I just don't understand it. I was asked here. I was given employment. Sam, too. So you see, Ben, we just got to stay."

"No matter what I say then, you're staying?"

"We have to, Ben. Right, Sam?"

Gila Sam shifted uncomfortably and cleared his throat. "That's right, Marshal."

"All right," said Ben. "But the first crooked move you make I'm going to jail you for a spell, then boot you out of town."

"Ben," Jim protested, "we're just two peaceable fellows trying to earn a living."

The marshal glanced from one to the other, then he turned and stalked out.

"Ben's looking old," said Jim, making the delayed turn. "King wins. Trey loses. Yes sir, he's looking damned old." Now he glanced up at Juan Alvarez, who had backed the king and was collecting. "What kind of a town is this, mister? I walk in minding my own business and marshal wants to kick me out."

"Mr. Gann's very strict," said Juan. "It was just a warning."

Jim laughed. "And Doc Sprigge operating right across the street? And I've been told he carved his initials on one of the customers so hard the man hasn't spoken a word since."

"Self-defense," said Juan. "Doc was up before Judge Howard for it."

"So? Wouldn't you fellows call that kind of a misdemeanor, to kill a man? Well, Doc's still here."

"That's not the marshal's fault," said Ballard, the gunsmith, speaking up.

Jim scratched his head in seeming perplexity. "Too deep for me, boys. Let's play."

* * *

It was nearly midnight. Luis Aranjo was standing at the corner of Howard Street and Deadman Creek Road, in the Mexican settlement, holding two guns on Blackbeard and Red, who were protesting that they hadn't done anything and that the greaser woman was crazy. But Luis knew the "greaser woman." She was a cousin of one of his friends. She was standing just beyond him, a plump, pretty little widow, about forty, sobbing and wringing her hands.

"Aw, come on, mister," said Blackbeard, "let us go. So we propositioned her. What's wrong in that?"

"Liar," cried the Mexican woman. "They followed me home. I tried to shut the door but the one with the red hair put his foot in it. Miguel Lopez—you know, Pete's boy, only fourteen—he came along and tried to help me and they kicked and hit him and he fell down. Then the one with the black beard, he grabbed me, tore my dress—"

"Yes, yes, Mrs. Garcia. Never mind. The marshal will be here in a minute. Be quiet now," cried Luis impatiently, never taking his eyes from the two men. It was sort of dark here and Luis was worried. It was obvious to him that this was a pair of real tough customers and not just a couple of more or less harmless strange Anglos who had sauntered into Mextown, looking for excitement and somebody to bully.

"He lied when he said I invited him," Mrs. Garcia went on, full of grievances and unable to stop talking. "He lied. He lied. You think I would have anything to do with such men? Impossible."

"Yes, yes," said Luis.

Now he noticed a look pass between the two men, a furtive, sidelong look. He moved back cautiously just as Red made a dive for him. Luis's move threw Red's lunge off and Luis brought the barrel of one of the .45's down on his head. Red fell on his face with a groan. But Blackbeard had drawn. Luis flung himself to the ground just as Blackbeard's gun went off. And then suddenly all was confusion, as Homer rushed in out of the darkness from some place and hit Blackbeard a resounding blow with the butt of his rifle. Blackbeard gave a loud gasp of pained surprise and fell forward on his face beside his pal.

Luis got to his feet, shaking. "By God, Homer—" he began.

But the marshal arrived at that moment and Luis never got to finish what he was going to say. Now someone came running with a lantern.

"Hold it over these two fellows," said the marshal.

The lantern was held over them. Grunting with distaste, the marshal turned Red and Blackbeard over with his foot, so roughly that they both groaned.

"Yeah, I know 'em," he said. "A couple of murderers from the hills south of here. God, even they're coming back in now. The one with the beard is called Shag. The red-headed one's name is Spence. We'll throw 'em in jail and hold 'em. Somebody may turn up with a warrant. Wish we could hang 'em to a tree out south of here and leave 'em there for the other boys from the hills to look at."

"They tried to attack Mrs. Garcia," said Luis.

"But didn't succeed?"

"No, thank God," said Luis. "The black-bearded one tried to kill me."

"That so," said Ben. "Well, maybe we can hang 'em yet."

He prodded them with his boot toe. "Come on. Come on," he said, impatiently. "What's a little knock on the head to beasts like you!"

Luis stooped down now and removed their guns. "Search 'em for knives," said the marshal.

Homer helped Luis in the search. "Phew!" Homer exclaimed. "These men stink."

Each man had a knife inside his shirt. Blackbeard's had bloodstains on it.

"Look at this, marshal," said Luis.

"I see," said the marshal. "But he could have been cutting meat with it. When they come to we'll parade 'em straight down Howard Street, and boys, if they don't move fast enough, kick 'em. May act as a lesson."

It was twelve-thirty now and the gambling room at the Palace was jammed to the walls. Doc dealt imperturbably, with a stogie clamped in the side of his mouth. Pinto seemed half asleep in the lookout's chair. Frenchy laughed and hummed to himself, keeping the cases.

Mule Casper hurried in to bring Doc some news. Doc was beginning to realize that the old burro-wrangler might come in handy with his long nose, so, noticing his frantic signs and his knowing grins, he motioned for him to come round the table. Mule's puny chest was puffed out as he moved into that sacrosanct spot.

"Lean over. Talk low," said Doc.

"By God, Doc," said Mule, sweating with excitement, "you should have seen Ben and his boys kicking them badmen all the way down Howard Street. Hell, it was like a parade. Fellows lined up on both sides."

"Anybody I know, I hope?" said Doc, laughing. "Not Long Jim Trahan!"

"No, a couple of filthy thieves from the hills, south," Mule went on. "Fellow called Shag and a fellow called Red Spence."

"Shag. Shag," said Doc, musingly. "I remember him. He's a grave-robber type. Morgan Earp hit him over the head with his cane and him wearing two guns and afraid to draw. Spence I don't know. So old Ben's getting rough. Hell, he ought to be in the Old Soldiers' and Sailors' home. Fought in the Mexican War—Civil War, too."

"Did you fight in the Civil War, Doc?" asked Mule, slavishly deferential.

"Me? I'm from the South. I ran," said Doc. "Clear to Baltimore. Studied medicine while all those fools were killing each other."

"I seen service," said Mule, eager to talk. "Camel Corps."

"*What?*" cried Doc.

"Sure enough," said Mule. "We had camels—in Florida. Didn't work out."

Doc was beginning to get bored with him. "Okay, Mule," he said. "Circulate. Don't miss anything."

"I sure won't, Doc. I sure won't."

Mule, grinning at anyone who would look at him, moved round the end of the table, then strutted into the bar for a drink before he went out on "reconnaisance again for Doc," as he said.

Ben took off his gun-belt and flung it aside with a disgusted grunt, then he sank down in a chair and sat staring off across the room. He felt old tonight, and looked it. "It's like trying to dip out the ocean with a sieve," he said aloud, then gave a slight start as a door opened behind him.

It riled him to be caught talking to himself and he spoke irritably. "Berta! What are you doing up?"

Berta came over to him and put her hand on his shoulder, but the shoulder felt so bony that she withdrew it at once, feeling a quick stab of pity. "He's got to eat more," she thought. "He hardly takes time nowadays."

"Cat got your tongue?" snapped Ben, turning around to look at her.

"Well, it was so hot I couldn't sleep," said Berta, "so I got up and dressed. Thought you might like some coffee so I made a fresh pot. Want some?"

"Yes," said Ben.

Berta brought the pot in, poured two cups, then sat down beside her father.

"Must have been busy tonight," she said, after a long silence. She wanted to talk. She wanted to ask Ben some important questions, but she did not know how to begin.

"Every night's Saturday night now," said Ben.

"Lot of arrests?"

"Twenty in the jail right now. All just drunks but two."

"These badmen—" Berta began, but broke off at once when Ben turned to look at her.

"Yes," he said. "What about them?"

"Well," said Berta, "are they all hopeless, do you think? I mean, if some of them had a chance . . ."

Ben laughed scornfully. "Who's stopping 'em from having a chance?"

"Well, I mean," said Berta, "suppose one of them would turn over a new leaf and get a regular job and just live like other people, what then?"

"Oh, they've tried it," said Ben. "It never works out. Berta, there are two kinds of men in the world. The builders and the destroyers. A man goes one way or the other because it's inside him. They can't switch back and forth."

Berta thought this over for a while. "Well, if that's true, Ben, then things are all pretty cut and dried, aren't they? I mean, we're just what we are. We have nothing to say about it. Like puppets, or something like that."

"More or less true," said Ben. "But it's a complicated question. Damned if I can see why you're bothering your head over it. Go to bed."

"I want to sit here with you, Ben, and talk," said Berta. She could remember when he used to take her on his knee, especially in the winter, and they'd sit in front of the fire and he'd tell her stories about when he was a boy riding on the riverboats and clearing land in Ohio in the 1830's. But Ben had changed. He'd changed greatly. He never seemed to want to talk to her any more. He just grunted. Grumbled. Barked out a word or two. The judge was right. The job was just too much for Ben at his age. It was slowly killing him.

"Shall I take your boots off?" she asked.

Ben looked at her angrily. "You think I can't take my own boots off?"

Berta recoiled and stared at her father in surprise. "Why, I used to take them off every night."

"You were a little girl then," said Ben. "It was just something you wanted to do. Go to bed."

"I'll finish my coffee. You want some more?"

"No," said Ben.

At three-thirty old Mule Casper hurried into the gambling room at the Palace, came around the end of the faro table, and whispered to Doc at length. Doc's face slowly turned red and his dark eyes glowed with anger.

"Great big sign," said Mule.

"What does it say again?"

"It's right on the front of the Nugget, and it says: FARO—HONEST DEALER."

Doc motioned for Pinto to take his place, then he went out into the bar with Mule and called one of the bartenders aside. "Eph," he said, "got any black paint around here?"

"Let me think, Doc." He snapped his fingers. "Yes. We been painting some signs—you know, like for the orchestra and—"

"Yes, yes," said Doc, impatiently. "Get it for me."

In a few minutes, Doc was crossing the street toward the Nugget, with his coat off and wearing two .45's strapped to his thighs. Behind him came Mule Casper carrying the paint bucket and brush, followed by a crowd of loungers, who didn't know what it was all about, but decided they weren't going to miss anything that had to do with the antics of Doc Sprigge.

Doc stopped on the sidewalk and with his hands on his hips regarded the sign sardonically. "As a solid citizen and property-owner of San Ygnacio I can't stand for this," he cried, to loud laughter; then he took the brush from Mule Casper, dipped it into the paint and carefully painted the letters D . . . I . . . S before the "honest" in the sign.

There were hoots, yells, and guffaws from the crowd. Hats were tossed into the air. And Doc, waiting for the uproar to bring results, got tired of waiting, finally, and walked back to the Palace, followed by a laughing, pushing crowd. Mule walked beside Doc, proudly carrying the paint bucket and the brush.

Chuckling to himself, Doc returned to the table and dealt in his shirtsleeves and wearing the two guns. Some of the players hadn't heard the story yet and were eyeing Doc mistrustfully. He hardly looked like his ordinary dapper self, heeled that way.

It was after four now. The lights were being put out in the bar and gambling room, and Doc, followed by Frenchy, Pinto, and Mule Casper, were just emerging from the Palace into the almost deserted street.

"By God, look here," cried Mule, pulling Doc's sleeve.

The big wooden sign was now hanging on the front of the Palace with its legend: FARO—DISHONEST DEALER plainly visible.

"Why, that son-of-a-bitch!" cried Doc, and then, jerking his guns with lightning speed, he riddled the sign, the sound of the shots echoing loudly through the deserted streets and bringing people up out of their blankets.

"Frenchy," called Doc.

"Yes, Doc."

"Take what's left of that sign and throw it through the front window of the Nugget."

"Okay. *Oui*," said Frenchy, calmly, gathering up the splintered boards.

Mule, Doc, and Pinto stood at the curb waiting for the crash. Suddenly it came, a violent shattering sound, followed by the faint tinkle of broken glass.

"Good thing everybody's gone home over there," said Doc. "Or there might be some fun in the street tonight."

VIII

But by noon the next day the big front window of the Nugget had been replaced, and the usual daytime calm had settled down over San Ygnacio. The Apache Rock stagecoach arrived, bursting with passengers but none of any particular consequence, Mule Casper noticed with disgust, and he only half listened to the shotgun messenger who was telling the crowd of hangers-on that a feeble attempt at a holdup had been made ten miles west of Ferguson's Ranch. "Amateurs, amateurs," the messenger said, patting his heavy-gauge repeating rifle.

"Shore carry yourself an arsenal," said somebody, indicating the messenger's rifle, shotgun, and revolvers.

The messenger laughed. His name was Bob Gall, and he was a grizzled veteran of the frontier. ("And a bigger liar than old long-haired Pap Drayer," Mule Casper thought.) "Oh, it's like hunting ducks," said Bob Gall. "I'll bring me home a brace of 'em yet, so the marshal can hang 'em up to age. Not that they need aging, most of them boys. They're right gamy as it is."

Mule finally shrugged in disgust as the messenger, stimulated by the interest of the crowd, talked on and on, then he went back across the street to his usual stand in front of the Long Horn Hotel. But it was an empty day, Mule decided, and getting restless he began to prowl the streets.

He even stopped to watch a dogfight, which was finally broken up by Homer Smith, who sent the curs flying with a series of well-aimed kicks.

"Getting pretty tame when the deputy has to interfere in a dogfight," Mule said, and Homer grinned.

"Marshal's orders," said Homer. "He don't like dogfights. Lots of hungry animals coming in from the south where them hillmen live. Don't know what they want with dogs in the first place. Won't feed 'em."

Mule stood shaking his head. "I don't know what's come over old Ben. He ought to retire and let this here town roar and run wide open. There ain't been one like it in some time."

"Marshal says it's the last," said Homer, "then we'll have some civilization."

Mule grunted. "If that's what he wants, why don't he move back East? He'd get a bellyful."

Homer grinned at old Mule and passed on.

"Oh, well," said Mule. "I think I'll get my dinner."

He strolled into Mattie's, expecting nothing, but right before his eyes there at the counter was Jim Trahan, wolfing down his eggs and bacon. He was in shirtsleeves and wearing two guns.

"Morning," said Mule, sitting down, one seat away from him.

Jim glanced at him, but said nothing. Jim's eyes were bloodshot, his face drawn and pale.

Mule shrugged, ordered his dinner from the Mexican boy who worked behind the counter, then sat humming an old Civil War marching tune to himself, tapping out the drum-rhythm with his fingers.

Suddenly Jim shouted at him: "Stop that!"

Mule stopped, then took off his hat and carefully scratched his thick mat of grizzly-gray hair.

"Put your hat back on," said Jim. "You think I want lice running around the counter?"

Mule meekly obeyed, inwardly amused.

"You know what you are?" said Jim. "You are a damned old nuisance, bore, and meddler. You keep out of my business, understand? Or I'll kick your carcass all the way to Deadman Creek."

"Is that friendly?" asked Mule.

Jim fumed, pushed his plate away, threw a silver dollar on the bar and stood up. He raised his right hand and, with finger poised, was just about to give Mule a dressing down when somebody came in the front door.

"Trahan!"

It was the marshal's harsh voice, and old Mule turned, grinning.

"Hi, Ben."

The marshal's face looked hard as flint.

"I heard about that little ruckus last night," said Ben. "And I been looking for Doc all morning. I'll find him. Now listen to me. Keep the peace. I'm warning you. Keep the peace."

Fury showed in Jim's face, but he controlled it.

"I'll do my share as well as a man can, Ben. But with that bastard—"

"I'm not arguing with you," said Ben. "I'm telling you."

He glared at Jim for a moment, then turned and left.

Jim snapped his fingers in a rage and kicked at a chair. "Crazy old fool!" he muttered.

Mule sat still as a mouse.

"And as for you, you damned old meddler!" Jim yelled, then he cuffed Mule on the side of the head and Mule's hat went spinning.

The Mexican boy's face turned white and he retreated toward the kitchen.

Mule spoke quietly. "That temper of yours will be the death of you yet, Jim."

Jim laughed wildly, then with one movement of his big

hand swept his dirty dishes off the counter. They smashed on the floor.

Big fat Mattie came hurrying in, pushing the Mexican boy aside. "You big ox!" she yelled. "What do you think you're doing? I'll get my broom and knock your ears off!"

The smashing of the dishes seemed to have eased Jim somewhat. He threw back his head and laughed, then he took out a five-dollar bill and tossed it on the counter. "There," he said. "Stock up the place. So you're Mattie."

The fat woman stared at him with compressed lips. "I don't even want to know who you are," she said, "because you ain't going to be here long enough to matter. All I need do is tell the marshal about this and he'll kick your fat ass out of town."

"Lady!" said Jim, as if horrified. "Such language!"

"I talk to people in the language I think they'll understand."

Jim laughed again. "Mattie, you're all right."

Turning, he hitched his gun-belt around, glanced at Mule, and went out. Now Mule retrieved his hat and began to dust it.

"Well, I never!" said Mattie, staring.

"That's Jim Trahan, the gun-fighter," said Mule, putting his hat on.

"Is that so?" said Mattie, unimpressed. "I don't see how he has lived this long."

"You want to hear a secret?" asked Mule, chuckling. "I don't think he's going to live much longer."

"Oh, that's too bad," said Mattie, with eleborate sarcasm.

The marshal finally ran into Doc as Doc was coming out of the Long Horn.

"Hi, Ben."

Ben did not greet him, but in a series of short, sharp sentences warned him to keep the peace.

Doc, who seemed relaxed and friendly, stood shaking his

head. "It beats me how things get around in this town," he said. "Just a little horseplay, Marshal. High spirits."

Ben stood looking at Doc with his thumbs hooked in his gun-belt. "You been warned."

"Yes," said Doc, "I been warned. You've done your duty, Ben."

"What I'd like to do, Doc," said the marshal, "is march you both straight down Howard Street and boot you out into the open country."

"I hear you did that last night to a couple of rowdies, Ben."

But Ben went right on: "Judge Howard won't hear of it. I just want you to know it's not my forbearance."

"Oh, I never thought it was," said Doc, smiling. "Look, Ben. You've said it all now. Let's go have a drink."

But the marshal glared, then turned on his heel and started back down Howard Street.

"Always forcing my hand, these fellows," thought Doc. "Too bad."

Shrugging, he walked across to the post office to see if there was any mail for him. A stagecoach was just making up. The driver stood aside at the sight of Doc, and spoke to him respectfully. Doc nodded absent-mindedly and went into the office. Staff was at the Wells Fargo window, dispatching a package for Pop Urbey.

"Hi," said Doc.

"Hi."

"Where do you keep yourself?" asked Doc, leaning on the counter beside him.

"I work," said Staff.

"Between ourselves, I'm going to place you yet," said Doc. "Just between ourselves. I respect a man's incognito."

"That's big of you, Doc," said Staff, mildly, then he got busy with the clerk, signing papers.

Doc turned away, dissatisfied, and walked over to the

post-office counter. "Goddamn it," he thought. "Couldn't he show a little friendliness?"

Night fell over San Ygnacio. The lights came on, one by one, then in clusters. Honky-tonk pianos began to play along Howard Street. And a delicate-looking crescent moon, the color of a muskmelon, came up over the hills to the east. To the south, coyote voices rose on the night, serenading the risen moon.

Time passed. Both the Nugget and the Palace were packed. There was no trouble of any kind. But the patrons of the Nugget noticed that Long Jim Trahan's face had a touch of grayish pallor. And the patrons of the Palace noticed that Doc was not his usual smiling and talkative self, but dealt in silence with a stogie clamped in the corner of his mouth. And an odd thing happened, which further unsettled the Palace patrons. A newcomer protested to Doc that Frenchy was not keeping the cases properly. Men began to draw back from the table, expecting another "Wilford" episode. The man had just lost. Doc declared it a win, without so much as looking up at the newcomer, shoved the money to him, and said in a mild voice: "There you are. Go play across the street."

The fellow left the table, looking bewildered. In the bar, he heard for the first time that the dealer was Doc Sprigge. He almost fainted. Pale and sweating, he hurried back and abjectly apologized to Doc, saying he must have been mistaken. Doc nodded and accepted his further play without comment.

But at a little after eleven-thirty, Mule Casper came rushing into the Palace and, without an invitation or even a look from Doc, hurried around the edge of the faro table and leaned down.

111

"Doc," he said, "they got a new sign made—and they put it on the front of the Palace."

"What does it say?"

"It says: FARO: DISHONEST DEALER—all painted up new, bigger than the other one."

Doc smiled to himself, stroked his chin for a moment, then said in a very low voice: "Always forcing my hand."

"What was that, Doc?" asked Mule.

But Doc ignored him and rose. "Gentlemen," he said, "I've got to leave the game. But Pony Willis and Leo Trotter will be glad to carry on, if you like. Thank you all."

Doc disappeared into a little back room, followed by Pinto and Frenchy. Mule was coming in, too, but Frenchy said: "Go 'way. Private business," and shut the door in his face.

Doc took off his coat and hung it over the back of a chair; then he reached his gun-belt down from a peg on the wall and buckled it on. "Pinto," he said, "tie those thongs for me—tight."

Pinto knelt down to tie the holster-thongs to Doc's thighs.

"Boys," said Doc, "if it comes, and I'm sure it's going to, let me make the play by myself. It'll make things easier afterwards."

"But, Doc," Frenchy protested, "two to one."

"Fair odds," said Doc, laughing. "Of course, if they get me, then use your own judgment."

Pinto had finished with the thongs.

"How's that, Doc?" he asked, looking up.

Doc tried a couple of practice draws and both Frenchy and Pinto watched him with admiration. "Tighten the right one a little," said Doc.

Pinto bent down again.

"Frenchy, you take the sign and throw it through the window," said Doc, "then get back across the street fast."

"How's that?" asked Pinto, tapping the right thong.

Doc made a lightning draw, and his "boys" laughed.

"I guess it'll do," said Doc.

Now Pinto and Frenchy began to get ready, taking off their coats, buckling on the fighting gun-belts that they never wore in the gambling room, and tying the thongs.

As they worked, Doc was saying: "I'll stand in the street just beyond the curb in front of the Palace. It's a wide street and if Jim tenses up, which he usually does, and starts shooting too fast, he won't even be able to hit the front of the Palace with that gun-fanning, let alone me. Frenchy, you stay down by those hitchracks below the Palace, and, Pinto, you move up the other way, toward the corner. And don't touch your guns. This is my night to howl."

Frenchy and Pinto both looked worried, but they nodded in agreement.

"All right," said Doc. "Out of the alleyway. We don't want a whole lot of hoosiers following us through the bar, yelling and carrying on."

They reached the front of the Palace without being observed. Men were passing in both directions, but they merely stared and went on. Not so Mule. He was waiting, and grinned at Doc and his "boys."

"I kinda figured . . ." he began.

But Doc cut him off impatiently. "Yes, yes! All right, Frenchy."

Frenchy, strong as a bear, ripped the sign from the front of the Palace and carried it across the street, staggering a little, as it was big, unwieldy, awkward to carry.

With his hands hanging loosely at his sides, Doc took up the position he had indicated, and Pinto moved reluctantly up toward the corner, looking back over his shoulder at Doc. Passing men glanced at Doc curiously, couldn't figure out why he was standing in the street that way, but finally shrugged and went on.

There were several loungers in front of the Nugget. They stared at Frenchy, openmouthed, as he staggered up onto the wooden sidewalk carrying the sign, and when, with a loud groan of effort, he heaved it through the big glass window, they turned and ran. The crash was terrific. Frenchy retreated rapidly back across the street at an angle toward the hitchracks of Gordon's Saloon.

Now Doc yelled in a wild, strident voice: "Everybody hit cover! Everybody hit cover!"

There were gasps of dismay all along Howard Street. "It's Doc Sprigge," cried somebody. "There's going to be a fight." Men ran in all directions like ants in an overturned ant hill; they dove into doorways, alleys, and open saloon doors. In a moment the street was as clean as if it had been swept by a giant's broom. Only Frenchy, Pinto, Doc, and Mule Casper were left.

Mule was chuckling to himself. "Blamed cowards! I wouldn't miss this for my right arm." He flattened himself into a shallow niche caused by the unevenness of two buildings. He had little or no protection, but it seemed enough to him.

Howard Street had grown very quiet. The saloon pianos broke off, one by one. Now loud yelling and arguing could be heard in the Nugget, but finally silence fell. A man came out, looked across the street, dashed back again.

Doc planted his feet wider apart, waited. Somebody was slowly opening the big swinging doors of the Nugget inward, inch by inch. In a moment, Gila Sam and Long Jim Trahan both slipped out at once. Jim turned to the right, Sam to the left.

"There's Doc," yelled Sam, then he drew and fired, missing.

Doc drew both of his guns and Pinto was sweating blood at the time he was taking. Sam fired again, missing. Then Doc took careful aim and shot him through the chest. Sam gave a loud cry, grabbed at himself, took a few running steps out into the street, then fell on his face, his hat rolling some distance.

Jim Trahan, moving cautiously beyond the hitchrack to

the east of the Nugget, fanned his righthand gun at Doc, the bullets kicking up the dust of Howard Street and ricocheting wildly with the shrill, insane shrieking.

Doc fired twice at Jim. Both bullets took effect, one in the left leg, one in the right hand. The righthand gun went flying and landed six feet away. Staggering badly and supporting himself against the hitchrack, Jim jerked his lefthand gun. But Doc, taking a long, slow, deliberate aim, shot him through the head. Jim jumped like a fish on a line, then doubled over the railing of the hitchrack, slid along it slowly, a dead weight, and fell heavily at the end of it into the alleyway.

Doc slid his guns back into the holsters, then he took off his hat and mopped his brow. Pinto, Frenchy, and old Mule hurried to him at once, laughing and crowing.

"Seven shots, no hits," cried Mule. "Four shots, four hits. Yippee!" Mule took off his battered old hat and waved it wildly.

Doc sighed. "I don't know what the West's coming to," he said. "Hasn't it got anything better to offer than Jim Trahan?"

At that moment, Staff came around the edge of the building. He and Pop had heard the firing at the corral, which was not more than two hundred feet away from the place where Doc had taken up his stand, and Pop was dying of curiosity. Staff pulled up at once at the sight of Doc.

Men were pouring out from every place now, and groups had formed around the bodies of Gila Sam and Long Jim Trahan.

Staff looked off at the two groups, then he looked at Doc.

"Hi," said Doc.

Staff walked over to him slowly. "Two on one?" he asked.

Doc nodded. "Got a witness, too. Maybe more than one—aside from my boys."

"Gila Sam fired the first shot," said Mule. "I was right here. I seen the whole thing. And Jim Trahan was fanning."

"Good shooting, Doc," said Staff.

Doc shrugged. "It was too easy. They got nervous. They let me play it my own way."

"Yeah," said Staff. "That's always a mistake. Well, I'll be getting along."

"You're the damnedest fellow for leaving places," said Doc, resentfully.

Staff turned and went back around the edge of the building.

"Queer cuss, that boy," said Mule.

Now Doc was struck by a sudden thought. He turned to Pinto and Frenchy. "Come on, boys. Hotel for us. Old Ben's going to start prancing and I just haven't got the heart to shoot that poor old bugger tonight."

"You figure he might draw on you?" asked Mule.

"I figure so," said Doc.

He and his boys started away.

"I'll keep an eye out, Doc," said Mule. "If I hear anything I'll come up and tell you."

Doc came back, slipped a bill into Mule's calloused hand, patted him on the shoulder and said: "You been a big help, old man. A big help."

"Aw, you didn't need to do that, Doc," said Mule bashfully.

At this time, the marshal was helping Dr. Ortega in Mextown. For months there had been bad blood between two Mexican families, and tonight it had flared up into a knife fight. Three men had been pretty badly cut up and a fourth had fallen into Deadman Creek—where there was only a trickle of water from the spring rains, but plenty of big rocks—and got a concussion. While Ortega patched up the wounded, the marshal talked to the older members of both families. He laid the law down to them; he swore at them; he threatened to run them out of town; in short, as Dr. Ortega said, "he scared the hell out of them," and shortly had them eating out of his hand.

Later, other members of both families began to appear, and in a little while there was much weeping and kissing and hugging all around—and pretty soon, laughter.

Finally, wine was brought out and women hurried to the kitchens to cook up a "feast."

Exhausted, Ben and old Dr. Ortega, both successful in their ministrations, sank down on a bench in front of one of the feuding houses and lit their cigars.

The far northwestern edge of Mextown was a long ways from upper Howard Street, and the sound of the gun battle had not penetrated.

"Sometimes I'm ashamed of my people," said Dr. Ortega. "But I love them."

"They're warm-hearted," said Ben. "It's the cold-blooded of this world I can't stand. Like Doc Sprigge."

Ben and the doctor talked on quietly. The moon was half-down in the west now, hardly more than a silver shaving.

But as Ben and Dr. Ortega talked on, much action was taking place behind Ben's back. Rufe Caton reached the scene of the battle first. Len Cline came right on his heels. Realizing that this battle might mean a turning point in the history of San Ygnacio, Rufe sent Len on the run to report to Judge Howard and let him take what steps he thought were necessary. Meanwhile, he persuaded Homer Smith not to go running after the marshal. Homer was hard to persuade. But Luis Aranjo arrived in time to help Rufe keep Homer in check.

"Homer," he said, "you know what this means. The marshal will try to run Doc out of town."

And so, actually, Ben was not informed at all. He found out another way. Ray Reeb, one of the judge's "legitimate" clerks, came looking for Dr. Ortega, who was acting coroner. He started at the sight of the marshal, but it was too late to back down now, so he blurted out the whole thing.

Ben turned white, but said nothing.

"Two on one, Marshal," said Reeb, hastily. "And Gila Sam fired the first shot."

The marshal still said nothing.

The three of them left together for town.

"Marshal," said Reeb, sweating, nervous, "I understand the judge wants to talk to you before you take any action. He's at his office."

"All right," said Ben.

Pop was sitting at his desk, with a lantern burning at his elbow, drinking a glass of beer that Staff had brought in to him. Staff sat slumped in a straight chair near by, with his long legs stretched out and his hat down over his eyes.

"I guess thirty is not such a high figure after all, Staff," said Pop, reflectively. "He's already killed three here."

Staff made no reply. Picking up a straw off the floor, he began to chew on it. Pop glanced at him, noting his extreme preoccupation.

"How long do you think this can go on?" Pop asked, wanting Staff to talk to him.

Staff seemed not to hear. In a moment he stood up so abruptly that his chair gave a loud, shrill squeak, like a slate pencil on a slate, and Pop winced.

"Guess I'll go back uptown," said Staff. "See what's going on."

"You figure the marshal might—?"

"Yeah," said Staff, before Pop could finish his sentence. "He might."

Staff started out.

"Well," said Pop, "I'll be waiting to hear."

Staff gestured and disappeared.

"Now I wonder what's eating him?" Pop asked himself, then he relit his cigar and settled down rather discontentedly to his beer.

* * *

The door of the courtroom, flush with the street, was wide open to the desert night, laying a long beam of yellow light across the dark roadway. There was no wind, and the small American flag on the judge's desk hung limp. The judge, Mule Casper, Al Tweedy, Homer Smith, Len Cline, and Tom Wade, the judge's other "legitimate" clerk, were grouped round a table, with papers before them. Just beyond, the door of the judge's little office was open and Berta could be seen sitting at a desk and tapping nervously with a pencil.

The men talked in low tones and Tom Wade kept writing rapidly.

In a little while, boot-heels squeaked across the board sidewalk outside and they all turned rather apprehensively and looked. In a moment Ben Gann came in. His face was pale, his lips set.

"Am I intruding?" he asked.

Judge Howard coughed uncomfortably. "We couldn't find you, Ben. We had to act fast and—"

The marshal planted himself in one of the kitchen chairs beyond the railing and crossed his arms.

"Don't let me interfere with the due process of the law," he said. "But I don't suppose you mind if I sit in."

"Ben," said the judge, "stop it. Nobody's trying to exclude you."

"I just saw the bodies," said the marshal. "They're being moved now. And I also had quite a conversation with Pap Drayer, who was very drunk. You know what he said? He said he'd heard they were going to start a new graveyard because the old one is going to get too crowded if Doc Sprigge stays around here."

All the men looked very uncomfortable.

"Marshal," said Homer, "I wanted to run and get you right away, but I got talked down."

Ben snorted a laugh. "The 'clerks' have taken over, I guess," he said. "Who's bringing Doc in?"

"Why, young Rufe Caton," said the judge. "Since you

119

were busy, Ben, we thought it would be a good idea to get him in here as fast as possible."

The marshal laughed scornfully. "And I see you've been taking testimony. Another hearing, eh? Exoneration—is that it?"

"Would you like to hear some of the testimony, Ben?" asked the judge.

"Yes, I guess so."

"Mule?" prompted the judge.

"I saw the whole thing," said Mule, eagerly. "Marshal, it was a clear case of a man defending himself. Gila Sam shot first. In fact, he got in two shots before Doc was ready. Missed both times. Jim Trahan was fanning his gun before Doc fired a shot."

The marshal said nothing.

"And, Ben," said the judge, "Al Tweedy saw the whole fight—from the other side of the street. His testimony is exactly the same as Mule's."

Mule was a town character and not too much was thought of him, but Al Tweedy was a solid businessman, and managed the big general store for the Boggs family. His testimony was not to be laughed off.

"Did you hear, Ben?" asked the judge.

"I heard," said Ben. "Gentlemen, I warned Doc Sprigge only this afternoon to keep the peace."

"Well, blast it, Ben," cried Mule, "how could he keep the peace with men shooting at him?"

"I understand it was all about a sign," said the marshal. "Schoolboy stuff."

"No matter what it was about," said Al Tweedy, rather sharply, "two or three shots were taken at Doc before he fired."

Now Ben turned to the judge. "You figure, then, you'll have a hearing and just release him, is that right?"

"I don't see much point in a formal hearing," said the judge, "unless you've got some testimony that conflicts with what we have here."

The marshal laughed scornfully again, then for the first time he noticed Berta. He gave a slight start and rose. "Berta," he called, "what are you doing here? Come out of that office!"

Berta got up and came slowly and reluctantly into the courtroom.

"Len came and told me what happened," she said, with her eyes lowered, "so I just—well, walked over here to talk to the judge. I went to the jail first, but you weren't there. I was worried."

"All right," said Ben; "but what are you doing sitting around here now?"

"I asked her to stay," said the judge.

"Why?" snapped Ben.

"Well," said the judge, "if you want me to be frank, I expected trouble from you and I thought that Berta might be able to—"

But the marshal cut him off, breaking in—angrily. "Go home, Berta. The judge has been acquainted with us for a long time but apparently not long enough, or he would know better than to think that you would try to sway me, one way or another, in a matter like this. Am I right, Berta?"

"Yes, Ben," said Berta.

Now he spoke more gently. "All right, Berta. Go home."

She glanced about her rather uncomfortably, then crossed the little courtroom and went out through the open door. Then she gave a start. A tall man, who had apparently been listening to what was going on inside, had drawn back into the shadows, beyond the doorway. But now her heart gave a leap as she recognized the eccentric shape of the hat, silhouetted against the dim street lamp of the little side street.

"Staff!"

"Miss Berta," said Staff, taking off his hat.

"What are you doing here?" she asked, as she moved

121

away from the lighted doorway into the shadows beside Staff.

"Oh, just curiosity," said Staff.

Berta was surprised. Staff just did not seem to her like a man who would be lurking about in the dark, eavesdropping. She didn't know what to say.

"I heard what the marshal said to you," said Staff. "The judge was wrong, having you wait. But at home, couldn't you . . . I mean, kinda try maybe to make the marshal see it the judge's way?"

"No," said Berta. "And I don't know that I'd want to. It was just an idea of the judge's; sounded all right the way he put it. But as soon as I saw Ben come in, I knew it was just no good. This job is Ben's life—and he's got to handle it his own way."

"Pretty hard going it alone," said Staff, "with his own people not backing him. And then it's a touchy thing. You know. What they call the code of the West. Doc always fights that way, at least as far as I know. It always puts him in a good position with most of the men in a town. Mighty hard to argue against."

Berta sighed deeply. "There's just nothing I can do, Staff. You don't understand Ben. Of course, I could cry and carry on and argue, but that would just irritate him, make it worse."

Their hands touched in the darkness. Staff's hand jumped slightly, then came back to hers. He gripped her fingers and she returned the pressure, suddenly feeling all warm and young and alive, and forgetting, for a moment, that Ben was in serious trouble and that she was helpless to give him any aid.

"I wish there was something I could do," said Staff, in an altered voice. "But what? The marshal would throw me in jail if I tried to back his play. It would be like me saying I didn't think he knew his business."

"But why do you even consider—?" Berta began, then broke off. "I mean, it's not your fight, Staff. It's—well, things like this have been happening to Ben ever since I can remember. And you're right, Staff. He wouldn't *let* you help him. He's getting old—and he hates to admit it. He even got furious at me because I wanted to help him off with his boots. Maybe I shouldn't feel like this, but, well, Ben's just got to do it his own way, fight it out the way he sees it. He wouldn't be happy otherwise."

Their hands parted reluctantly and they stood there silent in the darkness, both wanting to say things they felt they should not say.

In a moment they heard footsteps and turned. Four men were coming toward them from the direction of Howard Street; they were mere black shapes while the glow from the doorway vaguely illuminated the faces of Berta and Staff. The men were close by, now.

"Well," said one of them in surprise, "Stafford!"

It was Doc Sprigge. He glanced quickly at Berta, then, smiling ironically, he passed on into the courtroom, followed by Rufe Caton—who looked at Berta curiously, then at Staff—and also by Sol Reed and Ross Bagley, the lawyer.

"He looks like a little gentleman," said Berta. "He doesn't really look awful at all."

"You better be getting on home, Miss Berta," said Staff, hurriedly. "I want to hear this out."

"I think I'll stay, too."

"I wouldn't if I were you," said Staff. "The marshal said for you to go along home. And suppose he'd come out and—?"

"Yes, yes," said Berta, quickly, "you're right. He's got enough on his mind without thinking I'm spying on him. Because—because he's getting old—and, well, the judge seems to think he can't handle his job any longer and even calls me in to help. That's what he'd think."

Their fingers touched again. Staff grasped her hand and pressed it gently. Berta responded with an answering pressure, then she took her hand away, turned, and hurried off down the street. Staff looked after her, and then moved closer to the doorway to listen.

The marshal had resumed his seat beyond the railing, as if to remove himself entirely from any complicity in what was being done and said in front of the judge's bench.

"I want to call your attention, Judge," Ross Bagley was saying, "to the fact that my client, Doc Sprigge, is appearing here voluntarily. Am I right, Rufe?"

"He's right, Judge," said Rufe. "I met them coming out of the hotel. They were on their way here."

Doc kept pulling at his tie. He'd had a few drinks, but not enough. He felt depressed and fidgety. From time to time he glanced over at Ben, but the marshal ignored him.

"I see," said the judge.

"The fight was forced on him, Judge," said Ross. "I think, if we needed to, that we could establish the fact that Mr. Shaker, owner of the Nugget, hired Jim Trahan to come in here and heckle him. For obvious reasons. Mr. Reed and Doc Sprigge were making too much money at the Palace to suit some folks around here. And there's another thing I'd like to establish. Certain people in this town like to picture Doc Sprigge as a fly-by-night, a drifter. But, Judge, Doc Sprigge is now part-owner of the Palace, a real propery owner, I might add, who has the best interests of this community at heart."

There was a brief silence. Surprise showed on all faces except the marshal's. He merely laughed scornfully. Doc glanced over at him but made no comment.

"So," said the lawyer, "if there is to be a hearing, let's proceed with it." He took a paper from his pocket and handed it to the judge. "Here's a list of witnesses, if more are needed."

Judge Howard took the paper and sat tapping it on the table.

"I hardly think we'll need these witnesses," said the judge. "In fact, I see little point in a hearing at all. I wasn't an eye-witness of the fight, but I haven't heard one word of conflicting testimony, so, if Marshal Gann has no objections, we'll just forget the whole thing."

He turned to look at Ben, who stood up. "I'm not going to try to tell you your business, Judge," he said. "You've got your function, I've got mine. I just want you to answer one question."

"What's that, Ben?"

"Do you want my badge?"

"No, no," cried the judge. "What are you talking about?"

"You want me to continue as marshal then?"

"Of course."

"You have complete faith in me?"

"Naturally."

"In that case you think I know how to maintain law and order in San Ygnacio and what is wrong and what is right for the peace of the town. Am I right?"

"Yes, yes," said the judge, beginning to show a decidedly worried face.

"All right," said Ben; now he turned to face Doc, Sol Reed, and Ross Bagley. "Doc, you're a very slick article. A property-owner, eh? What did you buy this property with—money or threats?"

"It's all legal," said Ross. "I'll show you the documents if you like."

"Very recent, wasn't it?"

"I don't see why we should answer that question. It has nothing to do with the matter in hand," said Ross.

Doc said nothing. He just pulled at his tie and fidgeted.

"I don't care whether you answer it or not," said Ben. "I just want Doc to know he's not fooling me any." Now Ben paused and looked at Doc, as if studying him, weighing him. "Doc, listen to me now, carefully. I warned you when you hit this town that at the first sign of trouble, out you went. I was overruled. In regard to the Trahan business, I warned you to keep the peace only this afternoon. I told you

125

what would happen if you didn't. Again I'm overruled. But this time I'm not going to stand for it. Doc, the Dayton Mills stagecoach leaves at ten a.m. tomorrow morning. Be on it, you understand? Be on it."

There was dead silence. Doc glanced at the men seated at the table, shrugged, pulled at his necktie.

"But, Ben—!" the judge protested, half rising.

"Do you want the badge?" snapped the marshal, reaching up to the front of his shirt.

"No—no," said the judge, sinking back.

"Good. All right, Doc—anything to say?"

Doc shrugged. "Why do you men always force my hand? You know my motto. Live and let live. Won't you sleep on this, Ben?"

The marshal turned and started out; he paused at the door and said harshly: "Dayton Mills stage. Ten a.m. Be on it." Then he went out.

He noticed a tall man leaning against the courtroom wall, smoking a cigarette, but he paid no attention and, hitching up his gun-belt, he started for upper Howard Street.

As soon as the marshal had disappeared into the shadows, Staff started back to the livery barn by a roundabout way.

In the courtroom, Ross was protesting: "But this is not legal. It's not even ethical."

The judge just sat shaking his head. Finally, Doc, showing mild irritation, turned and went out, followed by Sol Reed, who hadn't opened his mouth, and then by Ross Bagley, who was still protesting.

There was a brief silence, then the judge said, sighing: "With a man like cantankerous old Ben Gann, about all you can do is let him go to hell in his own way. I've done my best."

"He may make it stick," cried Homer. "He may make it stick."

But when he looked about the circle of men, they all lowered their eyes.

IX

"Can't nobody do anything with him?" asked Pop, relighting the stump of his cigar.

"No," said Staff. "It's got way beyond that." He paused and paced for a moment. "And he's right, from his standpoint. Irks hell out of him to see the others knuckling under to Doc. The marshal don't know what knuckling under means. Damn it all, Mr. Urbey, I admire that old man. He's tough. He's hard to down. But this time . . ." Staff broke off, sat down, and stared in silence at the floor where a narrow beam of light from the lantern showed the cracks and crevices of the old, termite-riddled wood, the dust, the cobwebs.

Pop's cigar went out again and with a look of distaste he tossed it aside. "No match for Doc, you don't think, then," he said.

"He'd have to get awful lucky, the marshal would," said Staff. "It could happen. But Doc's tricky as hell, a dead shot, and fast as lightning if he has to be. But from what I hear, he just let Gila Sam and Trahan shoot at him till he was ready, figuring they'd miss. Doc don't waste bullets."

"Well," said Pop, sighing with resignation, "I guess we'll just have to wait and see. It's going to be a long night."

There was a protracted silence. Pop got out a fresh cigar

and lit up. Staff, sitting forward with his elbows on his knees, meditatively rolled a cigarette, his big hat down over his eyes.

"Mr. Urbey," he said, finally, "the last thing in this world I am is a meddler. In the West a man should ask no questions of anyone, keep his own counsel, and mind his own business. That's what I've always done. But *this* time . . ." He broke off and sat smoking and staring down at the ruined flooring. A cockroach appeared from a crevice, ducked back in as if bothered by the light, then came out again and crossed the beam from the lantern, hurrying. Staff watched it idly until it had disappeared in the shadows under the desk.

Pop's head was almost obscured by a cloud of cigar smoke. But he was studying Staff carefully, not knowing what to say. Who was this tall young man, after all? For weeks now he'd been Pop's close friend and companion—a son, almost. And yet actually he knew absolutely nothing about him. Would just an average kind of fellow—which was what Staff seemed to be—even consider interfering in such a deadly business as this? Doc and Ben Gann were two of the toughest men in the West. Was Staff somebody important, hiding out? Was Doc right in his suspicions?

Pop gave a slight start. Staff was speaking to him. "Mr. Urbey, have you got any guns about the place?"

"Yes," said Pop, after he paused a moment to collect himself, "I got a gun." Now he opened one of the desk drawers, took out a little nickel-plated .32 and put it before him. "Here it is. Not much of a gun and hasn't been fired for years, but . . ."

"Is that the only gun around here?" asked Staff, dismissing the .32 with a glance.

"Yes," said Pop. "I don't go in much for firearms. Never did. Of course, in the old days, I used to wear 'em, same as everybody else. But I never fired one in anger." Pop chuckled sadly. It was the truth, though. He'd always been peaceably inclined.

"Mr. Urbey," said Staff, "you got to get me some guns. I can't go buying any. I might be seen and it would get around. You know Mr. Ballard well, don't you?"

"Yes," said Pop, beginning to feel a rising excitement.

"Couldn't you rout him out and buy me a pair of long-barreled .45's, with belt and holsters?"

"I could. I could," said Pop. "But what would I say to him?"

"Tell him you're sending out a bunch of horses you sold to one of the ranches and you want Pete Lopez to be well armed, the way things are. You might mention those two fellows that the marshal kicked down the street. Say there's a lot of them lurking to the south."

Pop rose and stood nodding thoughtfully. "Yes. I could do that."

"Tell him you're sending Pete out at dawn, that's why you're routing him out. I hate to ask you to do all this walking, Mr. Urbey, but—"

"Oh, hell, do me good," said Pop. "You been pampering me too much lately, Staff. Well, I'll get started. But listen, son, I'm going to feel mighty damned bad if I buy you these guns and then you go out and get yourself killed."

Staff laughed shortly. "It's a chance a man has to take," he said.

In Doc's room at the hotel it was almost like a wake. Doc was lying flat in the middle of his bed, staring up at the ceiling. And Pinto and Frenchy were sitting near by, smoking, and regarding him uneasily. The Doc was in a bad mood. Since the fight he'd drunk almost a quart of whisky and he'd got so the last hour or two that he wouldn't even talk to them. Wouldn't even answer a question.

They felt like a couple of small boys who had suddenly

been abandoned to their own devices and to the chill winds of this worrisome world by a formerly indulgent and able father. They hadn't even undressed, nor had Doc. Frenchy was still wearing his coat. They kept glancing at each other, afraid to talk, almost afraid to move for fear their creaking and rustling would annoy Doc, who had seemed almost insanely irritable until he'd sunk at last into this nearly coma-like silence. But he wasn't actually asleep. His eyes were open. A hand twitched from time to time. Once he languidly brushed at a fly that was pestering him.

All at once Doc sat up and cried: "That stupid old bastard," and both Frenchy and Pinto jumped, then Doc leaned over, picked up the whisky bottle and took a long pull. "If he thinks he's going to run me out of San Ygnacio he's crazy!" Doc went on, staring hard at Frenchy and Pinto. Now Doc swung his feet around and sat on the edge of the bed, facing them. "We're in clover. We got money falling out of our pockets. We got a big cut of the Palace. When the real boom starts we'll end up as millionaires. We might even have our own private car. How would you like to roll into San Francisco in our own private car, boys?"

Pinto and Frenchy began to grin and chuckle. This was more like it! "Fine! Fine! Great!" cried Pinto; and Frenchy shouted: *"Formidable! Énorme!"*

"Doc's been a rolling stone long enough," said Doc. "He's seen too many camps, too many rocky trails, too much desert and cactus. Doc is going to stay here and roll in dough. You understand?"

"Oh, we understand, Doc," said Pinto.

"No old billy goat with a badge is going to take all of this away from Doc," cried Doc. "He's been warned, he's been put on notice—even by the judge. The businessmen are not even with him. Why can't he be sensible? Why can't he back up and let well enough alone? No, he's got to go and get himself killed. For what?"

"Damn fool," grumbled Frenchy.

Doc got up and began to pace. "Clear case of self-defense. Two on one. And yet the old goat's not satisfied. If I fought an army he'd still want to throw me in jail, just because I'm Doc Sprigge. The thing is, Ben was the big man till I came in. That's about the gist of it."

There was a faint scratching at the door. Frenchy and Pinto froze.

"Go see who it is!" yelled Doc. "What the hell's the matter with you?"

Pinto took a gun out of the gun-belt that was hanging on the back of a chair, and moved cautiously to the door. "Who is it?"

"It's me," came Mule's voice. "I just thought I ought to report . . ."

Doc shrugged and grimaced, showing irritation, then suddenly he had a change of heart. "Let him in," he said. "This old desert rat gets around. Might know something."

Pinto opened the door and Mule came in grinning self-consciously.

"Hope I'm not disturbing you, Doc. But I'm about ready to hit the blankets so I thought I'd better report."

"Good," said Doc. "What's the news?"

"Well," said Mule, "not too much, but I just thought you ought to know. Story's all over town. I been in every damned bar on upper Howard and a few in Mextown. Hell of a lot of men won't sleep a wink tonight, waiting for morning. Oh, it's a big thing all over town. I even heard some betting going on. Three-to-one you'd take the marshal, Doc."

"Odds are too short," said Doc. "Ten-to-one's more like it."

Mule chuckled. "That's what I told 'em," he said. "I guess I spoiled a bet because some big fellow I never see before, he sure got riled at me. But this gray hair kinda protects me, Doc. It sure does."

Suddenly Doc remembered the marshal's gray hair and a

change came over his face that startled Mule, who said hastily: "I guess that's about all, Doc."

"Nothing else?" snapped Doc, looking to see if the whisky bottle was still on the floor.

Pleased and reassured by Doc's interest, Mule chuckled and stroked his beard. "Well," he drawled, "I just don't know what this town's a-coming to. You know old Pop Urbey at the livery barn?"

"Yes," said Doc.

"Well, doggone," said Mule, still chuckling, "I'm coming up San Juan and I see a light in Ballard's gun store. It's late, so I wonder what the hell is going on. I go to the window and look in, and there—dogged if it's not the truth!—is big old fat Pop Urbey buying him some guns."

Doc looked at Mule so strangely that Mule felt all thumbs again and moved hurriedly toward the door. "Just a—a kind of funny thing I thought you might . . ." he stammered.

"What kind of guns?" asked Doc, abruptly.

".45's, looked like—two of them—long-barreled. Gun-belt, too. Can you imagine?" Mule went on, emboldened by Doc's question. "Old Pop. Hell, a more peaceable man never lived. But, of course, with all this riffraff coming in from the hills south maybe Pop figures he ought to get some protection. Pop's place is loaded with fine horseflesh."

"All right, Mule," said Doc, hastily. "Thanks."

Mule went out grinning. Pinto shut the door after him and bolted it. Doc walked slowly over to the bed, sank down on the edge, picked up the whisky bottle and took a long pull; then he sat staring off across the room as if in a dream. Frenchy and Pinto watched him uneasily.

"That tall fellow's mighty friendly with the marshal's daughter," he said, as if talking to himself.

"What fellow, Doc?" asked Pinto.

"Why, that . . . that . . ." Doc began, then suddenly he gave a loud, strident cry and jumped to his feet, his face going a little pale, his eyes glowing. "Brazos!" he yelled.

"That's who he is. I knew I'd seen him. I knew he was a gun. Brazos! Oh, I got him now." He sat down again on the edge of the bed, thinking hard, his eyes glittering.

"Brazos?" said Pinto, confused. "You mean he's in this town? Why, Brazos rode with Billy. He was one of the few that got clear. You mean he's here, Doc?"

"He's here, all right," said Doc.

"Brazos?" said Frenchy. "Sure, I've heard of him. I just missed him once in northern New Mexico. I came in, he went out. There had been a big ruckus. Brazos had a gun fight with three men in a bar. Had them all down. One died, two got well. Sure, I've heard of him. He's here, Doc? When did he get in? You figure he's going to deal some place, like Trahan? Does he deal?"

Doc laughed scornfully. "Boys," he said, "remember the tall fellow that bought our horses?"

"Yeah. Sure," said Pinto.

"That was Brazos."

"Oh, the one you could never figure out. Oh, sure. So you've got him tagged now, Doc?"

"I've got him tagged."

Now Doc became very thoughtful. Resuming his seat on the edge of the bed, he sat slowly rubbing his chin and staring off across the room. Pinto and Frenchy watched him in silence, waiting for him to explain about Brazos, waiting for him to tell them what to think and what to do, if anything.

"I can't take any chances," said Doc, as if talking to himself. "There's just too much at stake. No. I can't take any chances—and I won't."

He broke off, then sat as before, lost in thought and slowly rubbing his chin. Pinto and Frenchy, glancing at each other from time to time, stood waiting patiently to be enlightened.

"Let me tell you about Brazos," said Doc, and Pinto and Frenchy squatted down on their haunches in front of him.

"This was eight-nine years ago. He couldn't have been more than nineteen at the time. Hell, I was pretty young myself then—thirty—thirty-one. It was at Fort Griffin—the Flats. I'd been dealing, but business was bad, so I took to playing poker with some of the men around there. Square poker— well, mostly—and every man for himself. Well, finally a young kid wanted to sit in one night. Eighteen, I'd say. We tried to chase him away, but he showed us quite a roll and so we let him in. He just did so-so, maybe dropped or won a hundred. The next night another young kid shows up, wants in. Even the first kid tries to chase him away. But he's got a roll, too. So we let him in. The game was ordinary; nothing much happened; no big winning or losing. Next night along comes another kid. Same thing. They looked like cowhands to me, all three of them. Rough clothes, sunburnt, talked ignorant. But three of them . . . It began to bother me, in spite of the fact that they were always wrangling with each other. So I asked the bartender about them. His name was Lively and he was an old-timer in those parts. He said he'd never seen any of them before, but judging from their horses and everything, he figured they were cowhands who'd got paid off and were looking for excitement. Lot of big Texas ranches not too far away from the Flats.

"The game got bigger all the time. Men even came from Dallas to try their luck. And all of a sudden one of these kids—called Zeke—began to win—*big!* And I began to lose—*big!* Now, I'm no sucker gambler and I started to get annoyed. So I began to cheat. I still lost, not so big, you understand, but I should have been winning. So I knew right away there was something wrong with the game. Well, I was alone down there then, but a couple of guys who were regulars seemed to me like they could take care of themselves if it came to trouble, so I took them aside and explained that we were all being cheated some way, and that it must be the three kids. They couldn't believe it at first.

134

But little by little I figured it out. These boys had signals. They played very conservative poker ordinarily. But when one of them got a hand, a big hand, he tipped it off to the others and they saw to it that there was a big pot. There was a lot of other finagling, too, that I won't go into. We were being taken—and by beardless boys.

"Well, the two other guys and I set it up for one Saturday night. We were going to teach the boys a lesson. The three of them came in separately and the game started. *We* had signals now, and not only that, we pulled some pretty terrible stuff, cheating barefaced. But the kids just pretended they didn't notice. All the same I could see they were getting nervous. Finally one of them went out, excused himself. This bothered me. But he came back right away and went on playing.

"Well, men kept coming in and going out of the bar, so I don't know how I happened to notice this tall kid. He was wearing two guns and lounging at the bar under the picture of a naked woman on a red couch. It was Brazos—and if you think he's thin now you should have seen him then. One of the three had gone out to get him, smelling trouble, but naturally I didn't know that then.

"Well, pretty soon the blowoff comes. Five aces turn up on the table. All three of us beat the kids to their guns. Now you understand Brazos was standing clear across the room, looking like he was minding his own business. The next thing we know he's shot out the lights and a chandelier comes smacking down right in the middle of the poker table. It's dark as pitch in the place and men are yelling and falling over chairs and tables. What a mess! By the time we get a light, the three kids have disappeared and also all the money on the poker table. Brazos has also disappeared.

"I was so damned mad that I felt like shooting somebody, anybody. But the man who owned the place came in from the back and yelled: 'Drinks on the house for everybody,' and naturally that calmed things down. But nobody wanted to play any more poker, so, feeling kind of jumpy, I sat down and started a game of solitaire. A fellow I hadn't seen since I'd left Dallas and who had just hit town came over and sat with me. 'Doc,' he said, laughing, 'don't you know any better than to play poker with boys like that?' 'Like what?' I asked. 'Hell, I thought you knew,' he said, staring at me hard. 'The one they called Chivvy—short for El Chivito—with the buck teeth sticking out, was Billy the Kid. The one who shot out the lights was Brazos, the best shot in New Mexico.' "

Frenchy and Pinto, listening avidly, hadn't said a word. "So that's the fellow at the livery barn," said Pinto, as Doc did not continue.

"Yeah," said Doc. "And what's he buying guns for?"

"But Mule said—" Pinto began.

Doc cut him off. "Never mind what Mule said. Boys, we're not taking any chances on losing this gold mine. We're just not taking any chances."

Frenchy and Pinto glanced at each other, but said nothing.

Pop had gone to bed and Staff could hear him snoring in the little storeroom just beyond the office. Poor old Mr. Urbey! Worn out from all the excitement and the walking. Staff smiled grimly to himself as he dropped oil on the holsters and carefully rubbed it in. Everything was too new and stiff and creaking to suit him. Earlier he had oiled and worked the guns over, loosening up the action. Not that they weren't good guns. Hell, they were the best, with terrific firepower, due to the unusually long barrels. Pop hadn't spared the horses any. He'd really put out some long green for that pair of guns.

Now Staff weighed the guns in his right hand, one after the other. Loaded, they felt considerably heavier—and good. Damned good! And Staff experienced a faint stab of guilt that the handling of these big weapons gave him such marked pleasure. Putting the guns back into the holsters he thought: "Roy would understand. He'd forgive me. Breaking my oath's not such a killing matter, anyway, not when it comes to a rattlesnake like Doc. Never could abide a man who fights with a knife!"

Now Staff hung the gun-belt over the back of a chair, then opened the top drawer in the desk and took a look at the old turnip of a silver watch that Pop kept there. A quarter after four.

"Better get a little sleep," thought Staff. "Doc'll be up early tomorrow. Long before ten o'clock I'm going to have a little talk with that man."

He moved the cot out from the wall, fixed his blankets, put out the lantern, kicked off his boots, and lay down. A deep silence throbbed all around him, punctuated by the faint stomping of sleepy horses in the barns. He heard a nightman moving about some place in the back and then little by little he began to doze, his half-formed thoughts turning to Berta and the feel of her warm, soft hand in the darkness outside Judge Howard's courtroom. And then suddenly he was riding with her out in the open country, and this time there was no Mrs. Graham along and no Red and Blackbeard to spoil the day and remind him of his own shortcomings and all his wrongdoing of the past. Berta's long red hair was blowing in the wind. They pushed their horses into a rack, then into a gallop. The wind rushed past them violently. The sky darkened. Was there going to be a storm? And then . . . all at once . . . what was that? A crash . . . lightning?

Staff woke with a jarring start. Long red tongues of flame were spitting at him from the darkness. His left leg felt shattered. A red-hot iron was drawn across his belly, then across the upper part of his chest. He rolled away from the pain and cried out, like a man being tortured. The sudden shifting of his weight overturned the rickety cot and he fell face down on the floor, with the cot on top of him. The long tongues of flame continued to spit from the doorway. Bullets hummed and sang, tearing into wood with a ripping screech and ricocheting from metal with a savage, whining sound. At last the firing ceased. Staff heard frantic footsteps—two men, running in staggered time, toward Howard Street. Then the world went black.

When he opened his eyes again, a lantern had been lit and Pop and Pete Lopez were bending down looking at him with horror.

"My God, Staff—" Pop was sobbing. "What in hell—?"

"I think my left ankle's broke," said Staff. "And I got it at least three times in the body. God, look at me bleeding."

"We got to get a doctor," said Pete.

"No," said Staff. "Get me out of here. They might be back. A wagon—Pete. Take me to Mextown. Then get Dr. Ortega. He'll keep still."

Pete stared and then turned and ran out to hitch up a wagon.

"Got anything I can tie myself up with, Mr. Urbey?" asked Staff.

"Some towels," cried Pop. "Okay?"

Staff nodded weakly. Pop left, puffing and talking to himself, and returned carrying a stack of old and ragged but clean towels.

Pale, half fainting, Pop helped Staff bind up his wounds, wincing and turning away when he saw the blood seeping through the towels.

"I can't walk," said Staff. "Pete'll need help."

"Jiminez and Manuel are on tonight."

"Warn 'em not to say a thing. Not to mention this. I just disappeared—walked away—you understand, Pop?"

"Yes, yes. But who—?"

"Doc," said Staff. "He's finally figured me out, knew I

was friendly with Miss Berta. He's smart. Smart as a fox. But if I make it, Pop—he's a *gone* fox, sooner or later."

Suddenly Staff collapsed into a dead faint. Pop didn't know what to do, but just ran around wringing his hands.

Dr. Ortega worked over Staff by candlelight in the kitchen of Pete Lopez's house on the edge of the deep draw known as Deadman Creek. Dawn showed faintly in the east—a wide band of yellow above the barren hills. Roosters were crowing all over the Mexican settlement.

Pop was lying on a couch with his face turned to the wall. Jiminez had gone back to look after the livery barn; Manuel and Pete were assisting Dr. Ortega.

"Well, there it is," said Dr. Ortega, holding up a small hunk of lead with his forceps. "Right out of the shoulder muscles. The other two just sort of skinned you and passed on. But that ankle's bad, Staff. You're not going to walk for a good long while."

"You understand, don't you, Doc? You understand?" Staff kept repeating, his face chalk-white.

"Sure, sure, we all understand," said Dr. Ortega. "You've told us enough."

"Don't go to the marshal," Staff insisted. "He's got enough trouble. Don't tell anybody. Nobody. I just run out. That's the story."

"Yes, yes. Quiet down now," said Dr. Ortega, "while I see what I can do with that ankle."

Dr. Ortega had used chloroform on Staff, who was now sleeping heavily.

"Well, Doc—?" asked Pop, who had been roused and was now drinking a cup of coffee.

"He should live unless he's lost too much blood."

"*Live!*" cried Pop, choking on his coffee.

"Yes," said the doctor. "You think he's just been stung by bees? He's got three body wounds, one of them pretty serious—and a broken ankle, with complications. If he's lucky he'll be up and around in a few weeks. If he's not, well, who knows?"

Pop groaned; then he said: "Doc, we've got to do as he says. We've got to."

Dr. Ortega glanced over at Staff's new guns and gun-belt hanging from a peg on the wall. "You mean he was going to tackle Doc Sprigge—that skinny young fellow?"

"Yes, yes," said Pop, "and he will yet. He wanted to protect the marshal."

"God bless him," said Dr. Ortega. "How do you suppose Doc found out?"

"Maybe I was seen buying the guns and Doc someway put two and two together. We don't know."

Dr. Ortega sat shaking his head. "God, this is a day I hate to see dawn. The marshal's just got to go it alone, I guess."

X

The marshal ate his breakfast in silence. It was a little after seven and it was going to be a hot day. The sun had cleared the hills to the east some time before, there wasn't a cloud in the sky, and heat shimmers could already be seen dancing over the dust of Howard Street. The doors and windows were wide open, but there wasn't even a suggestion of a breeze. The buildings across the way were casting long dark-blue shadows, as well defined as if they had been drawn with a sharp pencil, while the gaps between the buildings showed a whitish glare, hard on the eyes.

Berta tried to act as if she thought this was just another morning. Brushing her hair away from her forehead, she said: "It's hot already."

Ben nodded slowly, and chewed in silence, looking off beyond his daughter at a spot on the wall.

"More hot cakes, Ben?" asked Berta.

He merely shook his head, then tapped his coffee cup. Berta leaned across with the coffee-pot and poured his cup full.

"Good coffee," said Ben. "You're learning." Then he smiled at her.

There was a certain sweetness about the smile that surprised her. He hadn't smiled at her like that for years; not since she was a little girl.

"Well, thanks, Ben," she said.

"Apple pie tonight?" he asked.

Berta's lips trembled slightly. She hadn't given supper a thought. She cleared her throat before replying, trying to steady herself. "Yes, Ben. I found some very nice apples at Boggs's yesterday."

"Not too brown, now," said Ben, then he finished his coffee and rose.

Berta hesitated, then poured herself another cup of coffee. Ben, turned half away from her, was buckling on his gun-belt. She noticed that his hands were steady, but she also noticed that there was a certain stiffness about his movements, a certain rigidity in the way he held himself. . . . Age was creeping up on Ben, and in a few short years he'd be an old man like Pop Urbey, Colonel Drayer, and Mule Casper—sitting in the sun, unregarded by the younger men: a has-been, avoided by others if he was talkative, and largely ignored if he was silent. Ben would be one of the silent ones, proudly pretending that he did not know he was being ignored.

Ben reached for his hat and put it on.

"Well," he said, "I'll be on my way."

He turned and looked at Berta. His gray eyes seemed more faded than usual today, she thought. Rising quickly, she went to him, put her hands on his shoulders, and pecked him on the cheek. It was the daily ritual. But this time Ben did not recoil. His hands were on her back, and she felt a faint but convulsive movement. Suddenly Ben kissed her on the forehead.

"You're a good girl, Berta," he said. Then he turned quickly and went out, shutting the door behind him.

Berta stood listening to the sound of his boot-heels on the wooden sidewalk. Her lips were trembling and she fought for control. What could she do? What could she do? She had to help him.

Trying to calm herself, she cleared the table and began to

wash dishes. Her mind was in a turmoil. She couldn't think consecutively. The thought of a world without Ben frightened her badly—and yet—and yet—what was there for Ben to look forward to? Ben had his pride; it was about all he had left, except for herself. And this was his fight. No way to stop it, short of humiliating him and embittering him for the rest of his days.

She dried the last dish, then suddenly she whipped off her apron and ran out the front door into the street. Staff! She had to talk to him. Maybe he could think of a way to—to what? Prevent the fight? Back Ben up? But—no; that was the last thing . . .

She hesitated for a moment, badly confused. She even took a step back into the house. But at that moment she saw Homer come out of the jail and turn in her direction. Was he coming to the house? Had Ben sent him to look after her, while—? She couldn't stand the thought of Homer's slow, dull presence, in her agitated state of mind. She darted back between the houses, came out into the alley behind the courtroom and emerged into the little side street, where she'd talked with Staff the night before. It was deserted except for a few arrogant hens pecking in the dust.

"I've got to talk to Staff," she thought. "I've just got to."

When Berta entered the office of the livery barn, Jiminez and Pete Lopez were cleaning it out with mops and brooms. They looked up at her blankly, then took off their hats.

"Is—is Mr. Urbey here?" she asked, stammering with nervousness.

"No, ma'am," said Pete. "He won't be back till evening."

"Is Mr. Stafford here?" Berta could hardly bring it out. What was the matter with these two Mexicans? They were regarding her very oddly.

"No, ma'am," said Pete. "He's gone."

"Gone?" cried Berta. "Where has he gone?"

Pete lowered his eyes and stared at the broom he was holding as if he had just noticed it. "Nobody knows, ma'am," he said. "He just picked up and left. We don't know why."

Berta was stunned. She couldn't believe her ears. "Gone for good, you mean?"

"I guess so, Miss Berta," said Pete. "We don't really know."

"But doesn't Mr. Urbey know where he is?"

"No, ma'am," said Pete. "He—well, he was just as surprised as everybody else."

Berta didn't know what to say. She just stood there. Now little Jiminez bent down and began to wring the mop out into the pail. Pete scratched his head, carefully avoiding Berta's eyes.

"Wasn't this very sudden?" asked Berta, confused, unbelieving.

"It sure was, Miss Berta," said Pete. "Mr. Urbey had to go out on business on account of it."

Pete had been exhaustively prompted, but he was running out of lies and beginning to get nervous. Miss Berta's eyes were so blue and they blazed at you in such a funny kind of way!

"I just don't understand," said Berta, all at sea.

Pete remained silent, so Jiminez glanced up and said: "We no understand. Pete and me—we no understand."

Berta stood looking about her for a moment. Why were they cleaning up the office? This seemed rather strange. Pop Urbey was a very untidy old man. Why would he suddenly—? But almost immediately she dismissed this thought from her mind. What could it possibly have to do with Staff leaving?

Finally she turned, not knowing what to think or what to do. "Well, thank you," she said.

As soon as her footsteps had died away, Pete took out a bandanna and mopped his forehead.

"You got to lie better, Pete," said Jiminez, shrugging. "Talk like you meant it."

"I know, I know," said Pete. "But, poor Miss Berta—I hate to lie to her this morning."

"Sure," said Jiminez. "You think marshal—you think he—die?"

Pete nodded slowly, then he put his hat back on and began to sweep.

Berta had come to the livery barn roundabout, so that she wouldn't run into Ben, and she **was** returning the same way. Just as she neared lower Howard Street along a little roadway that wound and angled eccentrically, someone called to her, and she turned.

Homer was coming to her on the run, awkwardly swinging his rifle.

"Miss Berta!" he cried, panting. "Where you been? I been looking all over for you."

"I went out for a walk."

"The marshal wants you to stay home," said Homer. "I'm to stay with you. This is no day to be walking around the streets."

They crossed Howard Street side by side, in silence. Homer helped her at the curb.

"Maybe I could have a cup of coffee, Miss Berta," Homer said finally, rather apologetically.

"All right," said Berta, "come in."

They entered the marshal's house together. It seemed silent and deserted to Berta, and she went quickly to the kitchen and began to make fresh coffee. Suddenly she turned and went back to the sitting-room. Homer was rolling a cigarette, spilling tobacco; he looked up in surprise.

"Homer," said Berta, "has Ben got a chance, do you think?"

Homer shrugged. "Can't tell what might happen. Maybe Doc might decide to leave. I don't know, Miss Berta. But I'm not so down in the mouth as some people. I been following the marshal around for some time now. He's quite a man. Yes sir. Don't give up."

Berta went back to the kitchen. She felt helpless, and this terrible helplessness brought on a feeling of blank despair. The marshal fighting for his life. Staff mysteriously gone. Suddenly the world seemed to her like a very ugly and treacherous place. Why did these things have to be?

She leaned her forehead against the window-pane and cried quietly. But what good were tears? Could they help Ben? Could they bring Staff back?

Finally she got herself in hand and returned to the stove. Should she pray? She had not really prayed since she was a little girl; that is, prayed for anything for herself, only an occasional Our Father when she went to bed. She decided that she would not pray . . . at least, not yet.

She glanced at the kitchen clock. Five after eight. Two hours yet.

Shortly before nine, Pinto woke with a start. Frenchy was lying on his back beside him, snoring loudly. Cursing, Pinto rolled Frenchy over on his side. The snoring stopped. Pinto yawned and scratced, then he found a bent Mexican cigarette on the table beside him and lit up.

Doc's bed was empty, and Pinto noticed that the hall door was ajar. In a moment, Doc came into the room, carrying his shaving equipment and with his suspenders hanging.

"Morning, Doc," called Pinto.

Doc glared at him, said nothing. Pinto watched him as he put his stuff carefully away—Doc was so damned neat— and then began to finish with his dressing.

"Get up!" Doc called finally, and Pinto started, then began to shake Frenchy, who groaned and protested.

"Pinto," said Doc, "go circulate. See if you can find Mule Casper. *That* story ought to be all around town by now. But be careful. Don't ask him anything. Just let him talk. Frenchy can stay here."

Pinto dressed hurriedly and went out, his stomach rumbling with hunger. In the lobby, cooking smells tempted him but he knew better than to soldier on Doc—especially at a time like this.

In twenty minutes he was back. He looked baffled.

"Well? Well?" prodded Doc.

"I saw the old man," said Pinto. "He's been up since six o'clock. Hasn't heard a thing."

"What?" cried Doc. "Why, hell, I could hear the shooting right here in this hotel room."

"That's what he said."

Doc glanced at his watch irritably. "Hell, it's a quarter after nine. We haven't got much time. God, I wish I could depend on you two idiots. Now I got to go see for myself."

Trying to avoid notice, Doc hurried down San Juan Street to the livery barn. There was nobody in the office. He waited, then knocked loudly on the wooden wall and called: "Hey, anybody here?"

In a moment two Mexicans appeared—Pete and Jiminez. They started at the sight of Doc, then stiffened and held their ground, hatred making them brave.

"Where's Mr. Urbey?" asked Doc politely. "I'd like to see him."

Pete told the agreed-on lies. Jiminez was very pleased with Pete this time. He seemed so calm and natural.

"Oh, is that so?" said Doc. "Well, I can talk to Stafford then."

Pete replied as he'd been told to. Doc Sprigge seemed staggered, and Pete and Jiminez exulted in their hearts.

"Are you sure?" asked Doc.

"That is what Mr. Urbey said," said Pete, and Jiminez nodded.

147

Doc studied them, his face a little pale. "Were you two fellows here last night?"

Pete hesitated. "Yes, sir," he said; "we had a very busy night."

"Was Stafford here then?"

"I think so," said Pete. "He's always in and out. We work way in the back."

"Did he sleep here?"

"I think so," said Pete. "But he must have left awful early."

Doc pulled out a stogie, jammed it into his mouth and stood chewing on it. He looked both baffled and suspicious. Now he took out a twenty-dollar bill and showed it to Pete and Jiminez.

"If there's anything you can tell me, it's yours," he said.

Pete and Jiminez both shook their heads as if not understanding. "What could I tell you?" asked Pete, shrugging. "I've already told you all we know."

"That's right," said Jiminez.

Doc was convinced in spite of himself. They knew nothing. No Mexican stablehand that lived could resist the temptation of a twenty-dollar bill.

In a moment he turned on his heel and left.

Grinning, Jiminez patted Pete on the back. "That is the way," he said. "Me, I believed you, myself."

Pinto and Frenchy had their mouths wide open, staring at Doc in blank unbelief.

"But . . . but . . . but . . ." stammered Pinto.

"What were you shooting at, shadows?" cried Doc, his face pale, his eyes glittering.

"But I heard him yell. Ain't that right, Frenchy?" cried Pinto.

"Yes, yes," cried Frenchy. "He yelled very loud, like when a man is hit. Then we heard him fall. There was a big noise. Doc, I emptied both my guns. *Sacré chien*—is the man bewitched?"

Doc began to quiet down a little; then he stood rubbing his chin thoughtfully. "Of course," he said, "maybe they took him out and buried him and kept it dark. But why? Why?" He thought this over for a while. "Or maybe he was just badly shot up and they're hiding him. But why? Why didn't they call the marshal—report it? Why didn't it get around town? Goddamn it! None of this makes any sense at all. I just don't understand it." Now he turned and glared at Pinto and Frenchy. "You bungled it. Some way you bungled it."

"No," Pinto insisted; "it couldn't be, Doc. We hit him, and more than once you can bet. How could we miss in that little room? I tell you I heard him yell—and then there was a big crash."

Doc turned away and stood slowly rubbing his chin, lost in thought. Pinto and Frenchy began to grow very nervous. Doc was not himself. Doc was unsettled and jumpy. And this was no good, with the big showdown coming up, no good at all.

It was a quarter to ten. Staff lay in a coma on the little narrow bed at Pete Lopez's house. Pete's fat wife, Remedios, was sitting beside the bed, shooing the flies away from Staff with a palm-leaf fan. It was very hot, even in Pete's adobe house. The sun blazed in the narrow streets of the Mexican settlement. Men squatted in the shade with their big hats down over their eyes. Cur dogs lay panting, with their bluish tongues lolling out.

"Madre Dios," thought Pete's wife, "what will it be like in August?" Then she leaned over and looked at the tall, thin Anglo whose face was so pale and who was lying so still, almost as if dead. "Poor man! Look how he sweats."

Putting her fan aside, she rose and came back with a

dampened hand-towel and began to bathe Staff's face. His eyes opened. He stared at her unseeingly. She noted that his eyes were gray with little flecks of gold in them. He was a rather good-looking young man, Remedios decided, except that he was too thin.

Now she turned, at the sound of heavy footsteps. Old Mr. Urbey was just waddling into the room from the back.

"How is he?" he asked.

"The same," said Remedios, shrugging. "Look how pale he is."

Pop said nothing more. He sank down heavily into a chair, with a despairing groan, and just stared at Staff, shaking his head slowly.

Doc, in shirtsleeves, was strapping on his guns. Frenchy was at the front window; Pinto at the side window.

"Where is he now, Frenchy?" asked Doc.

"He's on the far corner. Just standing there."

Doc turned to Pinto. "How about the stagecoach?"

"People are still getting on," said Pinto. "Now the driver's climbing up. There goes the messenger with the shotgun. About ready to leave, Doc."

Now the guns were strapped on, the thongs tied, and, sighing, Doc walked over to the window beside Frenchy and looked down into the street, then he laughed sardonically. "Yep, there he is. Old Ben. With his ivory-handled guns. He's buffaloed many a character with them. A tough man, old Ben. Think how easy it would be for me to pot him from here and get the whole thing over with!"

"Shall I pot him, Doc?" asked Frenchy.

Doc snorted. "Thanks, Frenchy," he said. "But it's not as simple as that. They might hang you. No, I've got to do it according to Hoyle. Code of the West, you know, and all that nonsense. Though Ben will be just as dead. Boys, I'm going to tell you something. This is one I don't like."

Their heads jerked round. They stared at Doc in amazement. "Doc—!" Pinto protested. He felt uneasy.

"No," said Doc, "I don't like it. Maybe it's that gray hair that bothers me."

"But, Doc," cried Pinto, "think about all the money! Think about the Palace."

"I'm thinking—hard!" said Doc.

Now there was a loud hollering on San Juan Street, the cracking of a whip and the creaking and jolting of the Dayton Mills stage as it started out on the first leg of its grueling journey across deserts and barren hills and rocky, abrupt mountain roads.

"There she goes," cried Pinto. "That sure would have been one hot trip today, Doc."

Doc nodded slowly, then he said: "You boys stay out of this, understand? No matter what happens, stay out. As it is, I got the backing of a lot of people in this town who think that Ben is not giving me a fair shake, which he is not. Even the judge is on my side, legally speaking, that is. But if you fellows go to shooting and messing things up, then there'll be a quick switch. So come down with me to the lobby now and just sit there—understand?—till the thing's over. Nobody will be helping Ben. He wouldn't stand for it. It's man to man."

But suddenly a thought occurred to Doc that bothered him considerably. Staff! Had he got clean away? And would he have to tangle with him if the marshal went down? No, no; impossible. And yet the little doubt was there, as he went down the stairs between Frenchy and Pinto, who had become very quiet and subdued. They didn't like this business a little bit, not a little bit! What if something should happen to Doc? They shuddered at the thought.

They had reached the lobby. Several men, who were lounging there, made an elaborate pretense that they did not see Doc, and that they had no idea that anything was going on. Two of them hid behind newspapers.

"See them chairs?" asked Doc, pointing. "Plant yourself in them. Don't move till I come back."

Frenchy and Pinto sighed heavily, and reluctantly crossed to the chairs and sat down. Doc looked them over briefly, hesitated, hitched at his belt, started out, then stopped near the doorway. Through the big front windows of the hotel he could see the marshal crossing the street toward the stage station. Ben had no jacket on today. His greenish-black Stetson was tilted forward, over his eyes. Doc shook his head and sighed.

"Got a sprung behind, like an old man," he thought. "And look how his knees bend."

Pinto and Frenchy were leaning forward now, watching Doc. What was the matter? What the hell was the matter?

Now Doc hitched at his gun-belt again. Staff—Brazos—where the devil was he? What had happened to him? Doc swore violently to himself. "Get out there, you fool," he thought. "I know you got no stomach for it. But get out there."

Doc felt depressed. He couldn't hide it from himself. He felt goddamned low and depressed. His nerves, his muscles were not tightening up as they always did under circumstances like this. "What's the matter?" he asked himself. "You want to run? You want to hide?"

All along Howard Street men standing in doorways were talking nervously, and, like the loungers in the Long Horn Hotel, making an elaborate pretense that all was as usual on this hellishly hot spring morning.

An empty freight wagon lumbered east on San Juan, obscuring Doc's view of the marshal for a moment; but then it passed on, with the driver languidly cursing his team, and there again was Ben Gann, big as life, his hands dangling at his sides, waiting.

Doc steeled himself and stepped out onto the sidewalk, his eyes roving, to the left, to the right, and beyond the marshal, who had stiffened slightly. Doc felt nervous; and not in a good sense. He had an uneasy sensation that his back was badly exposed, that Brazos might—! But, good God, the idea was insane. He tried to kick it away from him as if it were a newspaper pasted to his leg by the wind.

Now the marshal called across the street to him. "Doc! I warned you!"

Doc said nothing. Far up Howard Street toward the Mexican settlement he saw men diving for safety. So . . . this . . . finally . . . was it!

And then it all happened in a split second. It happened so fast that if a spectator had blinked he would have missed the whole thing. Doc seemed to stumble slightly as he drew. But his draw was lightning; and it was matched across the street. Then came two shots, fired simultaneously; and, almost at once, the two men hit the ground, the marshal in front of the stage station, Doc in front of the Long Horn Hotel.

But Doc was up almost at once. His hat had fallen off and he was bleeding from a head wound. Frenchy and Pinto rushed out and helped him back into the hotel. Doc pushed them away, sank down into a lobby chair and took his head in his hands. The marshal's shot had barely nicked him. But Death had passed him only by inches; he had felt the clammy flapping of its black wings.

The marshal was lying stretched out in the street. He'd been shot through the right side of the body and his legs seemed to be paralyzed. He looked up grimly at the men surrounding him. "I knocked him down, by God," he crowed. "I knocked Doc Sprigge down."

"You sure did, Marshal," said Joe Ballard, who had come running up from his gun store just down the street.

Men rushed from all directions now, talking and gesticulating.

Mule Casper, who had watched the battle from the safety of the stage station, stood scratching his beard reflectively.

"By God, that was sure a surprise," he said to the mail

clerk. "Did you see Doc stumble? Even so, it's the first time Doc's ever been down. Well, I guess there's a first time for everything. Wonder how it feels to Doc? I remember the first time *I* got shot. It was in the leg. Couldn't get over how it could have happened to *me!* Made me right timid for a while."

Berta was crying and laughing at the same time. Ben was home, he was actually home, and lying in his bed. Dr. Ortega and Dr. Maynard were both with him now.

"He talked to me as if nothing had happened," she said to Homer, who was flying, and would hardly listen. "He smiled at me. He asked me if I was still going to have the apple pie. Imagine—as they carried him in!"

Homer swung at the air with a clenched fist. "He knocked him down. He knocked Doc Sprigge down. My God, what an old man he is! Damn it all, I'm a-going to get drunk tonight. Don't care if I end in jail. I'm a-going to get drunk."

Later, Dr. Maynard took Berta aside. "Berta," he said, "there's a good chance that Ben will get well. The shot went straight through him and the wound is no great problem. But . . . the bullet seems to have nicked his spine. We're not sure yet, you understand. It will take us a while to know. But, Berta, I just want you to realize—he may never walk again."

"I don't care," cried Berta. "Just so he lives. Just so he lives."

That night the Palace was jammed to the walls. Doc Sprigge was dealing with a bandage tied round his head. His thin lips were compressed, his eyes deadly. That afternoon, accompanied by Ross Bagley, he'd voluntarily turned himself in to the judge and had been released, but the judge's attitude had bothered him considerably. He thought that he had detected thinly veiled hatred and contempt.

On his way to the Palace that night he had encountered a drunken peace officer—one Homer Smith—who had brandished a rifle at him and called him a murderer. A couple of men managed to drag Homer away just in time to prevent Pinto and Frenchy from taking care of him.

Doc dealt mechanically, paying no attention to the players. "We bungled it all around," he kept thinking. "Pinto and Frenchy bungled it with Brazos. I bungled it with old Ben. I stumbled, for God's sake. What made me stumble?"

Doc was appalled. Such a thing had never happened to him before. Was his luck running out? When it was out, it was out. Like Hickok. Shot in the back of the head by a drunken nobody after winning fight after fight with name gun-slingers.

Doc tried to shrug it off. But one thought kept coming back insistently. He'd been downed for the first time—and by a man of sixty-five. It was damned humiliating.

Now Doc raised his eyes and ran them along the row of faces in front of him. No one met his gaze. What were they all thinking? He knew damned well what they were thinking. "Doc Sprigge—top gun in the West—he's been downed! *He's been downed!*"

XI

It was summer now. Although San Ygnacio sweltered under a blazing sun in a cloudless sky, far off to the west there were blue-black thunderheads over the mountains, an occasional faint flash of lightning, and a dull rumble of thunder. In San Ygnacio the air was powder-dry but full of electricity. You could see for miles. The hills looked as if you could reach out and touch them. To the northwest dust could be seen rising from the workings on the railroad spur, which was slowly moving closer and closer to the town.

But the loungers were paying no attention to any of this. They were massed at the corner of San Juan and Howard, watching a group of painters on a scaffolding, who, splashing paint recklessly, were using one whole wall of the Palace Saloon and Gambling Hall for their work. The loungers watched in silence as the brilliant, striking new sign—red letters on a yellow ground—began to take shape.

PALACE—SALOON, *GAMBLING*
Best in the West
DOC SPRIGGE—SOLE PROP.

A newly arrived lounger stopped at the corner and addressed himself to Mule Casper, who was a sort of leader in this shiftless, do-less group which daily milled through the town or sat in the sun on the steps of Boggs's general store.

"Did Sol leave?" he asked.

"Yes," said Mule. "Yesterday morning. Dayton Mills stage."

"Did Doc buy him out?"

Mule Casper chuckled. "Nobody knows. He bought him out or run him out, one."

"That Doc, he's getting to be quite a big man in this town, ain't he?"

"That he is," said Mule; "that he is."

Yes, Doc was quite a big man now. He'd bought a sprawling adobe house which looked off across the tableland at the far eastern end of San Juan Street. It was one of the oldest and largest houses in San Ygnacio and had once belonged to a high Mexican official who had lived there prior to the war with the United States. A fat old Mexican woman—Maddelena—kept house for Doc, and four or five of her sons were always hanging around the back of the place, eagerly running errands, carrying in wood, serving at table, or doing any other odd job that they could think of. They ate good at Doc's.

Pinto and Frenchy had a room of their own, and besides them, the house often swarmed with what Mule Casper called "retainers": Pony Willis and Leo Trotter, formerly of Tombstone; Guerra, a dubious Mexican from Sante Fe, who occasionally dealt in Doc's place and seldom said a word or even looked up at anybody; the Wardour brothers from God knows where—a couple of gaunt specimens, who claimed they had a mine in Gunnison, Colorado, and were now prospecting in the hills around San Ygnacio; and from time to time, others.

Doc's nightly progress from his home straight down San Juan Street to the Palace had become a familiar but interesting spectacle to the loungers of the town. They lined up for it, on the far side of San Juan, near Pop Urbey's livery barn. Doc was almost always punctual. At a little before nine he'd emerge from the house, followed by at least four men, sometimes more. Frenchy walked on one side of him, Pinto on the other.

Doc had changed, everybody decided; he'd changed a lot. His nervous walk had turned into a strut. He seemed slightly swollen somehow and moved forward with his chest thrown out, a little like a pouter pigeon. And the way he dressed! Doc had always been neat. Now he was a dandy. Some nights he'd appear in a white linen suit and a Panama hat. He'd discarded his boots long ago and now wore Congress gaiters, polished so they shone like a mirror.

He disdained to wear guns now and had even abandoned his shoulder-holster. "It spoils the set of my coat," he explained to Frenchy and Pinto, who hardly knew what to make of the new Doc.

Meanwhile, people poured into San Ygnacio from all directions as the spur neared the town. To the east a tent city was springing up; and in the town itself carpenters worked around the clock and constant hammering had become a familiar sound. There was hardly a quiet hour in the twenty-four.

Bob Gall, former Wells Fargo shotgun messenger, was now marshal and being a real old-timer did not take his duties too seriously. "Run it wide open, is what I say," he told anybody who would listen. He had six, sometimes eight and ten, deputies working for him, including Luis Aranjo, who spent all of his time in the Mexican settlement now and was seldom seen south of San Juan Street; Homer Smith, who had lost his enthusiasm since Ben Gann's retirement, seldom carried his rifle any more, and generally stayed at the jail where he acted as turnkey; Len Cline; and Rufe Caton, who was coming up fast and at the age of twenty-three was considered Bob Gall's likeliest successor.

Drunks were buffaloed and thrown in jail. "Beasts," like Red and Blackbeard, were given short shrift in the town and generally booted out without ceremony. The bars were expected to maintain a decent sort of order on their own or Bob Gall threatened to revoke their licenses. But on the whole there was little interference. Men like the Wardours and Guerra walked the streets unmolested, even unquestioned. Men wanted in other parts lived openly in San Ygnacio.

"She's just like Deadwood and Tombstone," Bob Gall explained. "And that's the way she'll be run. Old Ben . . . well, he should have known better, him having been around every place, but he tried to run it like a Sunday-school picnic. He couldn't move with the times. He couldn't realize that San Ygnacio was just not San Ygnacio any more—a sleepy Mexican town with a few Anglos. Hell, gentlemen, this here is going to be a metropolis."

So San Ygnacio roared on. From time to time there was a gun fight in the street, according to the Code of the West. Bob Gall looked on imperturbably, saw that the dead were buried, the wounded taken care of, and nobody arrested, or even brought in before the judge. "This ain't the East," he explained.

And through all this moved the resplendent figure of Doc, strutting in his white linen suit, his Panama hat, his red silk tie, and his black Congress gaiters with the mirror-like shine. He was a businessman now, a property-owner, a man of substance. Old-timers, coming in from all points, and hearing Doc was in town, rushed to say hello to him and then recoiled in surprise and awe. This—this was Doc Sprigge?

Doc was unchallenged. No more Jim Trahans showed up to heckle him and dispute his supremacy. Seedy gunslingers from all over the West talked to him politely and hinted that they wouldn't mind having a job, and maybe a loan. Doc helped those he liked—as for the rest, they left, after a very brief stay, at the suggestion of one of Doc's "retainers."

Doc kept a tight rein on his men. "We own the town," he

explained. "It's our town—understand? So we behave ourselves here. If you want to get drunk, get drunk at my house. And don't go looking for trouble—never. You can't get any higher than you are. Why spoil it? If trouble comes, that's different. We're respectable now, understand? Respectable."

Guerra never said a word to these admonitions. He didn't even nod or shrug. He was the best-behaved man of the outfit, and yet he had the reputation of being a deadly killer, with a long string of victims to his credit in Old Mexico and in the Sante Fe district.

No more was heard around town about Doc's surprisingly inconclusive encounter with Marshal Ben Gann. Doc was top dog—and that was that. Or so it seemed. But Doc himself—well, in spite of all his success, all the money rolling in, he could not fight off a feeling of uneasiness. Sometimes at night when he'd study the Palace books and realize how the money was piling up, he'd cross his fingers and knock wood.

"It's not natural," he'd think. "It's just not natural."

To the age of forty, Doc had been a drifter, hungry one day and with a bankroll the next—and then all at once—!

"It's just not natural," he told himself.

All the same, Doc rode his luck, like a real gambler. No concessions were made to the suckers at the table. If they didn't like the game they could go elsewhere. Frenchy, with a diamond pin in his tie now, kept the cases as before. "Gamble hungry," Doc kept instructing his men. "Gamble hungry."

Doc was a stripper at heart—a hit-and-run guy; and it was almost impossible for him to adjust himself to regular, lasting prosperity. He was an outsider, an outlaw—had been all his life. He could talk to his men all he pleased about being "respectable," but it was extremely hard for him to follow his own advice.

But this wasn't all of it. Brazos's mysterious disappearance still bothered him. Of course, now it seemed that either the fellow had been killed by Pinto and Frenchy and then secretly buried; or, wounded, had really taken a run-out for good when he realized that somebody was gunning for him with no holds barred. But still—!

Late one afternoon old Pop Urbey was greatly surprised and disturbed when he looked up and saw Doc standing in front of his desk. Just beyond him was a still-faced Mexican in Eastern store clothes and the pink-eyed one they called Pinto.

"Hi, Pop," said Doc, grinning. "Don't you ever gamble or drink or anything? Never see you around."

"Hard for me to get about. My arches," Pop explained. "And then I got varicose veins big as a gun-barrel in the back of my calves. I just sit."

Doc pulled up a chair and sat down, lit a stogie. Pinto and Guerra came in and stood with their backs to the wall, regarding Pop without interest. "Town sure is booming," said Doc.

"Sure is," said Pop. "My business has doubled, tripled maybe."

"What are you going to do with all that money?" asked Doc.

"What are you going to do with *yours*, Doc?" said Pop, wheezing a laugh.

"Oh, it'll get away from me," said Doc. "It always does." He looked about him meditatively. "So you're very busy, eh, Pop? I'll bet you miss that tall fellow. What was his name? He seemed to really know his business."

Fear stabbed at Pop briefly. He fumbled with his cigar for a moment to steady himself before replying. "I sure do," he said. "Pete Lopez is a good man, and all that, but Staff—he really knew horses and prices, and he was a good hand with the men. Got the best out of them without driving 'em."

"Never heard from him, eh?"

"Nope," said Pop, sadly, lowering his eyes. "Sure hurt my feelings, too. He was like a son to me."

"You never had any idea why he left?"

"Nope. Just a drifter, I guess. Paid him the day before, all he had coming. Maybe that was it."

"Yeah," said Doc, slowly, "maybe it was." Sighing, he rose and kicked back his chair, his leg acting automatically as he had seen Staff's leg act the second time he'd talked to him.

"Yeah," said Pop, "it hurt me. I liked that boy. Quiet. No trouble."

After a few more words, Doc left, followed by Pinto and Guerra. Pop waited until he heard them turn from the entrance into San Juan Street, then he took out a big bandanna and mopped his forehead. "This is not good," he said. "Not good at all."

As soon as it was dark, Pop put on his hat, walked back through the long series of barns and the corral, came out into an alley at the rear, and crossed upper Howard Street at its darkest point, near Deadman Creek.

Mrs. Lopez let him in with a smile, then she put her head out of the door and looked up and down to see if he was being followed. Too many people knew about the tall, thin Anglo. She was worried. Pete might get into bad trouble over it, bad trouble, with the town the way it was now, shooting, noise, streets crowded with dirty, tough-looking strange Anglos. Awful!

Staff rose to greet Pop, smiling. Pop saw his cane leaning against the wall. Staff was still lame but getting better every day. His face was pale, but he'd put on weight and no longer looked like walking death. In fact, due to Mrs. Lopez's cooking and his forced inactivity, he was at least ten pounds heavier than he'd been when he worked at the barns.

"Getting some meat on you," said Pop, sitting down with a heavy sigh and stretching out his legs to rest his feet.

"Hell, can't fasten my belt any more," said Staff. "I'll be plump as you, Mr. Urbey, if I don't look out."

Pop laughed, then grew serious and told Staff about Doc's visit.

"Good," said Staff, his mouth grim. "He's jumpy."

"I don't know," said Pop, shaking his head. "He's got this Mexican now, Guerra. You can tell he's a murderer just to look at him. Doc's always got four or five men with him now—all around him. It's like a procession when he goes to the Palace at night."

"That's what I said," Staff insisted. "He's jumpy."

Pop just sat shaking his head, sighing. He felt old, very old. Why didn't Staff just go away some place and forget Doc—live his own life? It wasn't worth it; it just wasn't worth it.

The marshal had tackled his disability just as he had tackled everything else in his long hard life, and to the astonishment of the doctors he was now able to pull himself out of bed with the aid of a chair and move about the house, leaning on one cane and using his free hand as a prop, against the wall, against tables and chairs and anything else that was handy. But it was very unlikely that he would ever be able to get about any better than this; his right leg was withered and shortened; and his back and neck were so stiff that it was almost impossible for him to turn his head.

Once seated in his big chair by the window in the dining-room, however, he looked like the Ben Gann of the past; in fact, maybe a little better. His color was good, his face did not look so taut and strained, and, like Staff, due to good food and forced inactivity, he had actually put on weight.

Berta was delighted with his progress and was now going into detail about it to Judge Howard who had come over after supper to "sit a spell with Ben." The judge listened absent-mindedly. He needed a shave. His linen was not quite clean. There were stains on his vest. And a strong smell of whisky about him. In fact, the judge was in a state of demoralization. He was still the mayor, still the only judge on the bench, but the town had completely slipped from his grasp. He was merely going along for the ride, as Marshal Bob Gall said, behind his back, and would probably be voted out of office at the next election, which was to take place in the fall, only a few months away. Ross Bagley, Doc Sprigge's lawyer, was getting to be the big man about town now, glad-handing all the newcomers, buying drinks promiscuously in all the bars, cultivating the Mexicans in Mextown, and telling them that as the original settlers of San Ygnacio they should have a larger voice in the running of the town.

There was nothing the judge could do about all this, and he knew it. Ross Bagley was loaded with money, probably Doc's; while he himself was a poor man, living on his meager salary as judge and mayor. He would soon be on the shelf with Ben Gann; but unlike Ben, he just could not be philosophical about it; he had no reserves. What could he do? Hang up a shingle and starve, as he had done all over the frontier as a young man? It would be pretty rough starting over again at fifty-five!

Berta kept right on talking about Ben's progress until finally Ben had had enough of it and said: "Berta, let's change the subject. You're boring the judge stiff."

The judge roused himself and coughed. He hadn't heard a word Berta had said for the last ten minutes, but he protested: "No, no. Not at all. It's almost like a miracle. Very interesting."

"Miracle, hell!" cried Ben. "I worked like a dog at it, from morning till night."

"Wore himself out," said Berta. "Almost died. Dr. Ortega lectured him by the hour. But he wouldn't listen. Just kept working at it."

"Even though I walk like a sidewinder," said Ben, "it's still walking. It's not laying in bed. Never could stand laying in bed."

The judge nodded wisely, his mind miles away. In a little while he'd go home, undress, get into bed, put the whisky bottle on the night table, and read one of the old novels that had been lying around his house unread for years, a legacy from a former law partner. The town would quiet down all around him. There would be nothing to distract him and remind him of his decline. And he'd be happy, happy—and drunk—till the dawn of a new day.

Now Luis Aranjo looked in at the open door, smiled, took off his hat.

"Well, Luis," cried Ben, delighted to see him, "come on in."

Luis came in and perched awkwardly on a straight chair. "How are you, Miss Berta? Judge? I hear you're walking pretty good, Marshal." He could never think of Ben as anything but "the marshal." His boss, Bob Gall, was just plain Mr. Gall to him.

"I manage to creep around like a crab," said Ben.

"Pretty soon you'll be walking good as new," said Luis. "We miss you."

"Why, thanks, Luis," said Ben. "And I miss the job—and all of you; but I can't complain."

"I got to be getting back," said Luis. "But there's something mighty interesting I thought you'd like to hear."

"What's that?" asked Ben.

Luis laughed, showing his even white teeth. "Well, Marshal, there are rumors flying all over Mextown that Billy the Kid is hiding out there and that he's laying for somebody."

Ben stared, then burst out laughing. The judge laughed also, but he was not exactly sure what had been said. Billy the Kid—something about *him?* Berta rose to get Luis a cup of coffee, but paused and turned, struck by a sudden wild thought. But, no, no—what was she thinking of? It was always Staff, Staff. She saw him in her dreams. She saw him just turning a corner, or passing on horseback far down on another street, when she was shopping. She saw him at night, passing her window, his hat pulled down over his eyes. She'd have to stop it. It was crazy. And now this wild thought!

"Billy the Kid," mused Ben, smiling. "Why, he's been dead for quite a few years now. Pat Garrett killed him. Matter of public record."

"Yes sir," said the judge, rousing himself, "matter of public record."

Luis laughed and shook his head. "You just can't convince the Mexicans of that. He was their favorite—El Chivito, you know—little goat. It's all over Mextown. There's talk in all the bars."

"What do you suppose started it?" asked Ben. "Just some drunk, making up a story?"

Berta had been listening in the kitchen. Now she hurried in with Luis's coffee, spilling some of it in the saucer. "Oh, I'm sorry, Luis," she said.

Luis was embarrassed at her concern. "If you want to know the truth, Miss Berta, I always drink it out of the saucer—like the marshal."

Ben laughed. "I don't think Berta approves of that, Luis."

But Berta wanted to hear more about the rumor. "Do you think that's it, Luis? Some drunk making up a story?"

"No, I don't," said Luis. "That's not the way rumors start in Mextown. They usually start when something is happening that they don't understand, so then they make up stories about it. It's my opinion that some young Anglo is hiding out. Maybe he's wanted by the law, and that's all there is to it."

Ben nodded. "You're probably right, Luis. Yes, that's logical."

Luis drank from his saucer, then smiled self-consciously. "Just thought it might be of interest to you, Marshal, as you can't get around town yet to hear things."

Berta was so agitated that she rose and went back to the kitchen. Could it be? Could it possibly be? But, no, that was crazy. "You must stop this!" she admonished herself severely.

It was a little after eight p.m. now and still very hot. Doc was sitting out in front of his house with his chair tipped back against an abode wall, fanning himself, and smoking a stogie. Pinto, Guerra, and Frenchy were sitting close by, smoking in silence.

The moon rose, big and yellow, over the hills to the east, and almost at once a breeze started to blow from the north, carrying a hint of moisture and coolness.

"Ah!" cried Doc. "Feel that? Maybe she'll cool off a little now."

"Evening, Doc," somebody called from the shadows.

Doc strained forward to look. Good God, old Mule! That old bore!

"Hi," said Doc, shortly.

Mule approached slowly and bashfully. Doc was much harder to contact now than he used to be. For a while Doc had been an easy source of ready cash. But, lately . . . well . . . Doc had so damned many people talking into his ear!

"Heard something kind of funny," said Mule, "that I thought might amuse you. Just kind of a joke, I guess. I don't know, though. Them Mexes are funny." Now he noticed Guerra, who had looked up quickly as Mule had mentioned "Mexes." "Oh, not you, Mr. Guerra," laughed Mule. "I mean the San Ygnacio Mexes. The peons."

"What is it, Mule? What is it?" demanded Doc, impatiently.

So, laughing and slapping his thigh, old Mule told Doc about the Billy the Kid rumor that was flying all over

Mextown. Frenchy and Pinto guffawed and even Guerra moved his lips slightly in what might have been a smile. But Doc did not seem amused; he did not seem amused at all. Taking out his wallet, he handed old Mule a bill.

"There you are," said Doc. "And keep your ears open."

Mule was astounded. He had been almost ashamed to approach Doc with that crazy Billy the Kid story. Need had driven him. But here he was with a bill in his hand—probably a ten or a twenty; there was nothing cheap about Doc Sprigge.

"Well, good night to you, Doc," said Mule. "And thanks."

As soon as Mule had disappeared into the shadows, Doc took Guerra aside for a private talk, much to the irritation of Frenchy and Pinto. In their opinion that goddamned greaser was getting too thick with Doc.

"The Billy the Kid thing is nonsense, of course," said Doc. "But there's something behind the rumor. There always is. In fact, Guerra, I'll level with you. There may be a man gunning for me hiding out in Mextown. You're a Mexican—you can talk the language—go see what you can find out. And if I'm right, don't wait. Take care of him."

Guerra was smoking a Mexican cigarette. The expression on his face did not change; he said nothing. The cigarette between his lips just moved slightly.

After a hard day at the livery barn, Pete Lopez was on his way home. He'd sort of taken Staff's place now and was no longer on the night shift. But the thought of home with his wife, Remedios, complaining about this and that as soon as he showed his face in the door was not exactly a delight to him at the moment, tired as he was, so he decided to stop into his favorite cantina for a drink or two. Nothing like a drink or two after work to ease the pain of living.

But as soon as he entered the little candle-lit place, he

gave a start and shrank back. Manuel—the little fool—was drunk and sitting at a table near the front with that Santa Fe killer of Doc's—that mass murderer from Old Mexico—Guerra.

Luckily Manuel had his back to the door. Pete eased up to the table sideways—it was near the end of the bar—and then turned his back on Manuel and began to gesture to the bartender. Manuel was laughing and talking a blue streak, bragging about his secret knowledge, and what a brave and foxy fellow he was—with Guerra egging him on. Pete listened with bated breath. And finally it came out—all of it. The shooting; the secrecy; the spiriting of Staff from the livery barn . . . all of it . . . all of it—in long-winded Spanish, with gestures. Now Guerra, cold-voiced, was probing for the most essential fact. Where was the man now? And finally, Manuel, after a period of coyness and kidding, told him.

Pete slipped round the bar and vanished. But in front of the cantina he paused. What would Guerra do? Would he go direct to the house? Or hurry back and consult with Doc? Pete thought for a moment; then made up his mind to a course of action. He squatted in front of the cantina and pulled his big hat down over his eyes, simulating one who had had too much to drink and did not want to go home. In a moment Guerra appeared. Pete began to sing drunkenly. Guerra threw him an irritated glance. Pete held his breath. Which way would Guerra go? To the left, toward town? Or to the right, toward Pete's own house where Staff was hiding? Guerra turned to the right.

Pete gave him a moment, then jumping up, he tore down the alley at the side of the cantina and made off into the darkness. Pete knew every alley, every short cut, in Mextown; he'd played all over the place as a boy. Shortly, he reached his own back door, panting, and burst in. Staff was sitting in the living-room, calmly drinking a cup of coffee, and listening to the troubles of Pete's wife. Two young boys and two young girls were sitting at Staff's feet, looking on in silence. Staff was a great favorite with Pete's kids.

Pete bounded across the room and whispered violently into Staff's ear. Staff's eyes flashed. And Remedios Lopez was astonished. It was what she called a "mean-Anglo" look, but she'd never seen it in Staff's eyes before.

Staff rose and buckled on his guns; then he limped rapidly to the back door and out, following Pete, who called over his shoulder: "Remedios, you and the kids sit still. Don't move."

It was pitch-dark at the back of Pete's house. Pete kept his hand on Staff's arm. "He's coming from that direction," he said, pointing. "So if you slip around the other side of the house . . . you'll meet him face to face with plenty of distance in between."

"Good," said Staff. "Now you go back in the house and keep out of this. Look after the missus and the kids."

"But Staff—" Pete protested.

"You do what I say," said Staff, coldly.

Pete hesitated, but finally he nodded and went back in, shutting the door quietly.

Staff slipped around the side of the house and stood close to the edge of the front wall, waiting, his hands hanging loosely at his sides. Very little time passed before he saw a dark shadow gliding up the street toward Pete's house. The man, Guerra, moved like an Indian, Staff decided: easily, effortlessly, and without a sound. If Staff had not been expecting him, he would not have known he was there. Guerra stopped, as if he smelled danger, looked about him for a moment, then came on more slowly. Staff gritted his teeth and waited. He wanted this man; he wanted him bad, and he was not going to let himself rush it and bungle things. Now he could see Guerra's white shirt front, a shadowy face.

Staff stepped out from the darkness abruptly. "You looking for me?" he yelled.

Guerra gave a jump and tried to throw himself behind a tree, drawing. But Staff was far too fast for him and got two direct hits on the white shirt front. Guerra fell with a clatter without getting off a shot.

There was a long wait. Staff approached the fallen man cautiously, keeping a gun on him. Now the two Montez brothers, who lived next to Pete and were in on the conspiracy, appeared, their opened door throwing a beam of yellow light across Guerra, who was lying on his back with his arms spread out. The Montez boys started violently when they saw who had been killed. Next Pete came running around the side of his house. He stopped dead when he saw Guerra's body.

"Drag him up between the houses," said Staff, "and put a blanket over him. I got a use for that fellow."

Pete and the two Montez boys obeyed in silence. When they came back Ruy Montez said:

"A bad one—Guerra. My father saw him one day in town and nearly fainted. My father worked in Santa Fe. Guerra killed many men there, and three women. Finally he had to run away to Old Mexico."

"Well, he won't kill any more," said Pete.

It was a little after four a.m. The streets of San Ygnacio were deserted and silent. The moon was down, the sky was faintly overcast and starless, and the street lamps at the corners looked dim, lonely, and inadequate, as if fighting a losing battle with the encroaching darkness. But in a moment the quiet was shattered by bursts of mingled masculine and feminine laughter, the big front door of the Palace was slammed back, and Doc and his retinue plunged out into the street. Doc, in his white linen suit, had a girl on each arm—one of them the big blonde, Tombstone Millie. Behind him came Frenchy and Pinto, Leo Trotter, Pony Willis, and the Wardour brothers, each with a girl. At the

171

corner of San Juan and Howard they whooped and hollered for a while, all talking at once, then Doc and his two girls started down San Juan toward his house, followed by the others. Millie, high as a kite, wanted to skip. Doc resisted for a moment, then gave in; and he and the two girls went skipping down the sidewalk, laughing and singing. Now all of them began to skip with their girls. Across from Pop Urbey's livery barn, Pat Wardour, big and awkward, fell full length, pulling his girl down with him. Hysterical screams of laughter rent the night. Pat's girl was pretty drunk and it was hard for Pat to get her up and started again, but finally he succeeded.

Up ahead, Doc was singing: "Gone again—Skip-to-maloo. Skip-to-maloo, my darling," all along the dark street. Doc was a graceful little fellow and at one time had been quite a dancer. He leaped lightly and in perfect time, hugging the girls tight and propelling them forward. The others straggled along behind, singing and skipping out of tune and time.

Doc's house was at the far eastern edge of town. There was no street lamp, and just beyond was the open desert. It was very dark. All of a sudden Tombstone Millie stopped dead and let out a shrill, hair-raising screech.

"What's the matter? What the hell's the matter?" yelled Doc.

"I—I—I stepped on something," stammered Millie, clutching Doc frantically. "It—it felt like a—a hand—"

"Maybe a toad," said Doc. "Just a toad."

The others had come up now. Cursing, Doc lit a match. Now all the girls shrieked at once. Guerra's body was lying across the wooden sidewalk in front of the entrance to Doc's house. The eyes were open, the white shirt front was covered with blood.

The men said nothing. The girls continued to shriek.

"Shut up! Shut up!" yelled Doc; then he turned to the

men: "Take the girls back. Frenchy and Pinto, you stay here with me."

Gradually the feminine uproar ceased. The Wardours, Leo, and Pony started back along San Juan, escorting the girls in silence. They had all been shocked into sobriety.

Frenchy kept lighting matches and looking down at the body of Guerra.

"What do you think, Doc?" asked Pinto.

Doc was calm now, maybe a little too calm, as if suffering from shock. "I don't know," he said. "I guess we'd better get the marshal."

Now lights blazed in every room in Doc's house. Leo, Pony, and the Wardours had returned and were sitting out in front, smoking in silence, while Doc, flanked by Frenchy and Pinto, was talking with Ben Gall and his little Mexican deputy, Luis.

"I don't know a damn thing about it," Doc was explaining. "Guerra took a walk about eight o'clock and that was the last any of us saw of him."

The marshal did not seem very perturbed or even very interested. He shrugged. "Well, Doc," he said, "no matter how you look at it, it's no great loss to anybody."

Dr. Ortega, the coroner, arrived, made a perfunctory examination, then the body of Guerra was carted off to the little morgue behind the jail.

To the east the sky was paling slightly, just a faint wash of lighter blue above the barren hills.

Now things had quieted down. Doc took off his hat and mopped his forehead, then he sat down with the silently smoking group.

"Had lots of enemies," said Pat Wardour.

"Yeah," said Doc.

Silence fell again. They all smoked. A dove-pale grayness began to show in the east.

Now there was yelling inside and they all started. In a moment Maddelena, wrapped in an old flowered robe, burst out the front door pulling one of her sons—Pio—by the ear.

"Tell the doctor, tell him," she cried, shaking him. Now she looked at Doc. "He saw; he heard. I just found out. Tell!"

Pio looked scared. Doc took him by the hand. "Okay, son," he said. "What is it?"

"It's not much," said Pio, shyly. "She gets too excited, Mama does. I was playing with José. It was late. We went to bed then sneaked out again. We saw these men riding in along the edge of town, from the north. Three men, leading a horse. We hid behind that big cottonwood tree. They stopped in front of the house, stayed there a minute or two, and then left. They never said a word. It was so dark we could hardly see anything. We got scared so we went back in the house."

Doc took a fifty-cent piece from his pocket and gave it to Pio. "Thanks, son," he said, then to Maddelena: "Take him back in."

Maddelena disappeared with her son, still admonishing him. As the door closed a loud slap and a yell of pain could be heard. One of the Wardours laughed shortly.

"Brought him in and dumped him here," said Doc.

"But who?" asked Pinto, bewildered.

"I don't know—yet," said Doc. But in his heart he knew. He knew only too well.

Dawn was showing now, a wide, fiery-red band above the cold dark blue of the hills.

Staff was just moving into a new hiding place and was saying good-by to Pete and shaking hands with him. Pete seemed distressed.

"This'll suit me fine," said Staff. "You got the missus

174

and kids to think about, Pete. And it may get bad. Another thing. No more Manuels."

"Oh, that little drunken fool," cried Pete. "I'm going to teach him a lesson with a buggy whip at the barn. He won't talk again."

"Nobody knows about this place but Pop, you, me, and the Montez boys," said Staff; then he turned and smiled at an old fat gray-haired Mexican who just stood there grinning; "and, of course, Uncle Julio."

Uncle Julio ran a poverty-stricken little racket store on the far northwestern edge of Mextown. He sold buttons, pencils, pins, needles, thread, and almost any other small and useful article you could think of. He slept in the back. Across from his cubbyhole was a shack with two bunks in it, where his brother, now dead, had slept for years.

Finally Pete left and Staff carried his gear into the bunkroom: a cane, a Winchester rifle, a gun-belt with two guns, several cartons of ammunition, and a saddle.

"You hokay, Billee?" asked Uncle Julio, grinning in the doorway.

Staff tossed his gear into the bunks, laughing. Pete had told him about the Billy the Kid rumor. And with the older Mexicans, like Uncle Julio, there was just no use in denying it.

"I'm fine, Uncle Julio, fine. Thanks. It's getting light. I better grab some sleep."

"*Si.* You sleep," said Uncle Julio. "I watch. I already sleep. You sleep now, Billee."

XII

Another hot summer day in the high tableland, with the sun pouring down a remorseless heat through a golden-yellow fog of dust. A whistling wind was blowing in from distant East Canyon, then fanning out across the flat tableland, whipping scrub bushes, raising whirling dustdevils which rose to twenty feet and then suddenly disintegrated, and catapulting big tumbleweeds that sailed and bounced in all directions, scarcely touching the ground.

Carrying several packages, Berta emerged from Boggs's general store into a strong gust of wind that was blowing straight down Howard Street. Her full skirt whipped about her, then ballooned, and, struggling with the packages and trying to hold her skirt down, she thought with regret of the jean pants she used to wear about the town before Ben had made her self-conscious with his talk.

"Miss Berta, Miss Berta," someone called.

She turned, still struggling. It was Luis Aranjo, and he was coming toward her on the run, his fat, dark face showing almost comical concern.

He came up to her, panting. "Let me take these packages. I saw you from way down the street. Sure is windy."

Luis took the packages and now Berta could use both hands on her skirt, which was flying, out of control. She looked about her in embarrassment at the loungers whittling and spitting tobacco juice on the store porch. But they all had their eyes lowered now. However, as soon as she looked away again, several of them smirked and raised their eyebrows at each other. As she reached the bottom of the steps she heard someone say: "Scenery sure is getting pretty around here."

She flushed and glanced at Luis, but he was showing an elaborately innocent face as he fell in step beside her.

"On my way to talk to the marshal, Miss Berta," he said. "Got some information I thought might interest him."

"Oh?" said Berta. "About what?"

"About that Billy the Kid rumor. There's a fellow hiding out, all right. But darned if I can figure out why."

Berta's lips moved a moment before she could ask her next question. "You mean, you know him?"

"Well, I know who he is," said Luis. "Used to be the foreman at Urbey's."

Berta's heart began to beat unevenly, almost wildly. "Are you sure, Luis?"

"Yes," said Luis, glancing at her. "I saw him."

Berta hesitated for a moment, then she said: "Luis, maybe you'd better tell me all about it and then I can tell the marshal. Ben—well, he's not feeling so—so very good this morning and—" She flushed at the lie she was telling and glanced at Luis to see if he had noticed it.

But Luis was too much in awe of her, too bemused by her mere presence, to notice anything except his own nervousness and lack of ease. "Oh, I'm sorry to hear that," said Luis. "You're right, Miss Berta. If I go and talk to him it might tire him. You're right."

"But you mustn't ever let on I told you," said Berta, getting in deeper and deeper. "You know how he is."

"Oh, I'd never say a thing, Miss Berta," said Luis, very pleased to be taken into her confidence.

There was a brief pause, then Berta said: "You say you saw him?"

"Yes," said Luis. "But I never ran into anything like this in Mextown before. What a cover-up! I know practically everybody there, you know, and I can usually find out anything I please. But not this time. Nobody would talk. Nobody! Till I happened to run across one of the Leon boys—about fifteen. I guess he hadn't been prompted or else he's just irresponsible. He told me a tall, thin Anglo was hiding out at Uncle Julio's on the far northwestern edge of Mextown—just a step from the open country. So I took a walk up that way. And sure enough there he was, out back at Uncle Julio's sawing wood, big as you please. As soon as he saw me he went back inside. Uncle Julio came out and talked to me. Sweet old man. Everybody loves him. Well, he denied that anybody was staying with him. Denied I'd seen anybody." Luis shook his head and laughed in a puzzled way.

"It was Staff? The man from Mr. Urbey's?" asked Berta, having a hard time controlling her voice.

"Yes," said Luis. "We don't want him for anything. And it's nobody's business where he stays. He could walk straight down Howard Street unmolested. I don't understand it. As you can see, there's nothing official about this at all, so I'm staying away from him from now on. But I just thought the marshal might enjoy hearing about it, since he can't get around town to catch all the talk the way he used to."

"Oh, yes," said Berta, "and I'll tell him all about it. And thanks, Luis, for coming to my rescue. I really had my hands full."

Luis returned the packages, then he took off his hat and made a little, awkward bow. "It was a pleasure, Miss Berta, a pleasure."

She gave him a sweet smile, then hurried round the corner out of the wind. Luis smiled after her, then sighed and started back up Howard Street. Miss Berta, what a fine, lovely girl, he thought; and without a single real beau.

Nobody around to her liking, obviously; and then, of course, the marshal was strict as hell with her, and rightly, Luis decided. She should be protected.

He ignored the wind, which was blowing dust in his face, and walked on, wishing that he was tall and slim, and not fat, and that his name was Louis Johnson, and not Luis Aranjo—even though he was half Scotch (and half water— oh, that stale old joke he'd had to listen to so often!)—and then maybe, just maybe . . . But what was the use of such thinking? After a struggle, Luis dismissed the whole business from his mind and tried to concentrate on the problems of Mextown.

As Berta came in the door, Ben, who was sitting by the dining-room window, called: "I'll bet that wind's rough on Howard Street."

Berta laughed and put her packages down. "Yes, it is, Ben. I was wishing for my jeans today."

Ben did not like such talk and eyed her severely. "See anybody? Talk to anybody? Hear anything?"

He was dying for information, for gossip. He had been an extremely active man all his life, talking with dozens of people daily, and having a hand in the civic affairs of many Western towns over the years. Although outwardly he seemed stoically to accept the new life that had been thrust on him, and never complained, in his heart he was restless and dissatisfied, and worked constantly, and sometimes in secret—hiding his efforts from Berta—at trying to improve his manner of moving about, hoping that eventually he could at least drag himself, without aid, as far as Boggs's general store, where he could sit with the loungers and listen to the talk.

"I just saw the people in the store," said Berta, avoiding his eyes, feeling very guilty. "Mr. Tweedy came and talked to me and asked after you, wanted to pay his respects."

Ben merely snorted. Al Tweedy—a spineless fool— backing Doc Sprigge up that night in the courtroom. He relit his pipe, stared out the window, said nothing.

"I'd better put these things away," said Berta, quickly. "Then I've got my ironing to do."

Ben grunted.

"But, child, what's the matter with you?" Mrs. Graham was asking. "Your face is red as a beet. Talk more slowly."

They were standing on the stoop of Colonel Drayer's house on Indian Road. It was after seven and growing dark.

"You've just got to help me," said Berta. "I told Ben I was coming over here for a visit. The judge's with him now, so that's all right. But if something would happen and he'd send over here for me, we went out for a walk—you must tell Mrs. Drayer that—and you've got to come along with me. Can you ride, dressed like that?"

"But—Berta—! What is it? It's almost dark. We can't go riding around . . ."

"It will only take half an hour, or maybe less. And don't worry about it being dark. Homer's going with us."

Mrs. Graham studied Berta's flushed, eager face for a moment. "Has it got anything to do with—?"

"Yes," said Berta.

"All right, then," said Mrs. Graham. "Don't worry. We'll arrange things. I'll help you."

Berta hugged her fiercely and began to cry.

"Here, here," said Mrs. Graham.

"I—I thought he'd gone away and I'd never see him again," sobbed Berta.

"Come on now, child," said Mrs. Graham. "Let's figure out what we are going to do."

The three of them were now riding through the desert at the far northwestern edge of the town, Homer, still bewildered but extremely glad to be of service to Miss Berta, a little in front, Berta and Mrs. Graham side by side.

Berta was very nervous and kept rubbing her hand over her hair and sighing. Was she acting like a fool? Ben would certainly think so. What was that he'd said to the judge? Something about no female being sensible; smart, yes, but not sensible—? "Well, I'm afraid he's right," Berta told herself. Several times she decided to turn back, several times she thought it might be better maybe to just send a note asking him when they could meet . . . but the three horses plodded on over the rough ground, on her left the scattered lights of San Ygnacio moved past slowly, the moon came up over the barren hills to the east, coyote voices rose on the night . . . time passed . . .

She came to herself with a start.

"See that little light, Miss Berta?" It was Homer talking. "That's Uncle Julio's. I don't know what this is about. I don't want to know. Marshal Gann will skin and flail me if he ever finds out, so the less I know, the better. The lady and I will wait right there under that big cottonwood tree. Don't be long, Miss Berta, or I'll have to come and get you. Doggone, I guess I owe the marshal a little loyalty." Homer sounded very plaintive, but, in some odd way, firm also.

"I won't be long, Homer," said Berta, hastily. "I'll be right back."

Uncle Julio was astonished to see this pretty, red-haired, excited-looking young Anglo female—a total stranger to him—who was talking so rapidly and, to Uncle Julio, so incoherently that he couldn't make out a word she was saying.

"*Si, si.* No, no," he said, confused. "I am just closing the store. Just closing."

"But I've got to see him!" cried Berta, taking Uncle Julio by the sleeve and shaking him gently.

Now the old Mexican's face lit up. "Billee? You like to see? Are you his *señorita?*" But before she could reply, his face fell and he shook his head sadly. "No, no. No one can see. He is not here. He has gone away."

Berta looked about her quickly, noticed an open back door and, beyond it, in a kind of hallway, a faint glow of light, then she brushed past Julio, who turned and made a halfhearted gesture to stop her. She gained the little hallway, but at the sound of her quick, light footsteps the glow went out and she was plunged at once into complete darkness. She gave a little faint scream; then she heard guarded movement down the hallway and, in a moment, a voice inquired: "Who is it?"

The voice was very cold. It was Staff, speaking as he had spoken that day at Mr. Urbey's when the little man—Doc Sprigge, she knew now—had come in unexpectedly.

"It's me," she said, hardly able to articulate; "Berta."

"Who?" Staff's voice sounded astonished.

"It's me—Berta Gann."

The glow sprang up again. It came apparently from a candle in a little room toward the back. And now Staff appeared in the doorway with a long-barreled .45 in his hand. He seemed to stagger slightly at the sight of Berta all alone.

"Miss Berta!" he cried. "What are you doing here?"

"I—I came to see you," said Berta. "Luis Aranjo told me—"

"He was lurking around here this morning," said Staff. "Is he going around telling everybody?"

Berta hurried to the doorway and stood looking up at Staff. "No, I'm sure he's not," she said, speaking very fast, very nervously, through emotional pressure and agitation. "I told him I would tell Ben and that's all Luis was interested in. He says it's not an official matter at all and nobody's business. Of course, I didn't tell Ben."

Staff just stood looking at her. Beyond him was the candle in a beer bottle on a box. She caught a quick glimpse of two bunks, of a coat and gun-belt hanging on a peg, a rifle, a saddle.

"Why did you leave?" she asked. "You might at least have told me."

"There was some trouble," said Staff. "Anyway, it's best for you to stay out of this, Miss Berta."

"Stop calling me Miss Berta," cried Berta, so sharply that Staff recoiled and stared at her in silence, not knowing what to say.

Berta hesitated, then stepped past Staff into the little bunkroom. Staff politely stood aside, then suddenly realizing that he still had the gun in his hand he reached out a long arm and shoved it back into the holster hanging on the wall.

They stood looking at each other in the flickering orange light of the candle; then suddenly Berta was in his arms and he was kissing her as if it was the most natural thing in the world. And down the dark hallway, Uncle Julio was craning forward to listen, and he grinned to himself at the long silence, and thought: "Billee's *señorita*. I knew. *Es verdad*. Is also hokay."

Now Staff drew back and looked at Berta as if he'd never seen her before. He was stunned. She seemed so eager for his kisses, so anxious for his arms to stay around her. This lovely red-haired girl! This ladylike young creature! It was almost like a miracle to Staff. What did she see so special in him? And now he drew back, suddenly remembering his not-too-clean cotton shirt, the stubble on his chin, his limp, his general unprepossessingness.

"I thought I'd never see you again," said Berta.

"Might be better if you hadn't," said Staff.

But Berta merely laughed at him. "I'm not going to listen to any more such talk from you," she said.

Staff looked at her in surprise. "What do you mean, Miss Berta?"

"Berta!" she insisted. "Berta! Remember?"

"All right, Berta," said Staff, beginning to grin. "You sure gave me one big surprise."

"Coming here, you mean?"

"Partly," said Staff. "Yes sir. You're a real surprise to me."

"Why? Because I let you know how I feel? What else could I do? You listened to Ben. You ran away every time I saw you. You told me a long story to warn me off. Then you disappeared."

"You sure are hard to discourage, Berta," said Staff, grinning. "Just like your father, old Ben—damn but he was a hard man to discourage. I guess Doc Sprigge knows that now."

"Well, now we've got that settled," said Berta, "what do we do?"

Staff hesitated for a long time, then he said: "Well, here's what I was aiming to do. There's a little business here in San Ygnacio I've got to take care of—serious business—and if it comes out all right I was figuring on leaving."

"And if it doesn't come out all right?"

"Well, I might have to stay here permanently, whether I wanted to or not."

Berta studied his face for a moment. "You mean you might—like Ben—?"

"Yes," said Staff. Then he went on: "Berta, you're Ben Gann's daughter so I know I can talk to you. A certain man in this town tried to murder me and he almost did. He didn't give me any chance at all. He just had a couple of his fellows sneak in and blaze away at me while I was sleeping. I got shot up pretty good and I had to hide till I was okay again. Well, I still got a limp, but that's no great matter, so I'm about ready."

"And then—you're going to leave?" asked Berta.

"That was the idea. It may be quite a fight, Berta, as I'm going to give this man a chance. I can't do it any other way."

184

"Staff," said Berta, firmly, "why don't you stay here and work for Mr. Urbey?"

"I'd like to," said Staff. "Nothing better. I love that old man. But I was figuring—after what Marshal Gann said to me and all—that it might be a good idea for me to get on out of here."

"On account of me?"

"Yes," said Staff.

Berta laughed at him.

"Oh, it's a serious matter," said Staff. "With my record, the marshal he'd never . . ."

"I can't help that," said Berta. "I made up my mind on the way over here, if it was really you, I was going to live my own life. Ben means well; but he just doesn't understand."

"He understands, don't you ever think different," said Staff. "The thing is he's just never seen a fellow like me turn over a new leaf and make it stick. I think I could. But I wouldn't swear it. Damned if I'd swear it."

"Nevertheless," said Berta, "if you go away from here, I'm going, too, so you'd better stay—on account of Ben."

"You mean you'd leave your father?" Staff demanded, astonished.

"If you left, I'd have to, wouldn't I?"

Staff was badly confused by this feminine logic. "Damn it, I don't know," he said. "I got the greatest respect in the world for Marshal Gann. Damn it all, he's a real man, tangling with Doc Sprigge at his age."

"Then stay," said Berta, and once again Staff felt confused by the feminine logic. It seemed all right, but what had been the objection to him staying in the first place? He felt all mixed up.

And there was no chance for him to get straightened out again, because Berta had come into his arms unexpectedly and he was kissing her and it seemed as natural and right as it had before—and also, strangely enough, like a miracle—

and he knew that he was just not thinking straight and, what was worse, he didn't give a good goddamn whether he was or not. Berta was so soft and sweet and she smelled so good he could hardly stand it. But all at once he drew back and, reaching out, quickly snuffed the candle. Then he put his hand over Berta's mouth.

"Shh!" he whispered. "Don't move."

Now she heard the cautious, guarded footsteps approaching the shack from the back. The footsteps hesitated, then came on again. Staff suddenly threw her to the floor, then flung himself down beside her. Two violent, jarring reports shook the shack and then it was so silent that they could hear dust falling all about them. "Don't move," hissed Staff, holding her down. Just as he spoke, there were two more loud reports, a board fell from the wall with a clatter, and little humming insects seemed to be all about them in the darkness. Again the silence, with the dust falling. Then they heard loud, frantic running, a fall, then more frantic running which, little by little, diminished into the distance.

Now Staff helped Berta to her feet. "You all right?" he asked, patting her awkwardly.

"What was *that?*" she demanded, her voice trembling. "What *was* it?"

"A coward with two double-barreled shotguns," said Staff. "He was so scared he bungled the whole thing." He put his arms around her and held her gently to him. "Berta," he said, "I got to move tonight. I was figuring I'd wait a few days. But this hiding is no good any more. Town's too small."

"Is—is that the way it was done before?" asked Berta.

"Sort of," said Staff. "Only I was asleep on a cot. The cot fell over on top of me and saved my life."

"You've just got to settle this man," said Berta, harshly, sounding like a feminine Ben Gann.

"Oh, I'll settle him, or him me," said Staff, "and in public."

"And then you'll leave?"

"No," said Staff, "I'll stay—if the marshal will . . ."

Berta kissed him. "We'll worry about Ben later," she said. "Now I've got to go."

He was proud of her as he'd been that day in the open country when Red and Blackbeard had frightened the daylights out of that poor lady, Mrs. Graham. Berta had taken it like Ben Gann's daughter should. And now this thing—and her taking it much better than any nineteen-year-old girl would be expected to!

They heard Uncle Julio puffing down the hallway. *"Madre Dios!"* he was moaning. "What was it, Billee? They try kill you?"

"It's all right, Uncle Julio," said Staff. "Now the young lady's leaving. Would you walk her home? I can't. Too dangerous for her to be with me."

But Berta explained that Mrs. Graham and Homer were waiting for her, just across the way at the big cottonwood.

"The peace officer?" asked Staff. "See that he don't report that shooting, will you, Berta?"

He kissed her again; she clung to him, then turned and hurried away.

"Got to move, Uncle Julio," said Staff. "Right away. Can you send somebody over to tell the Montez brothers to meet me at the little gulch? They'll know."

"I go. I go," said Julio. "They crazy man try kill you, Billee?"

"No," said Staff. "Just scared, Uncle Julio, just scared."

"Like to frightened the life out of me," Homer was moaning, as they rode back south along the edge of town. "What in tarnation was it, Miss Berta? Seemed mighty close to Uncle Julio's. I could see flashes."

"It was away beyond," said Berta.

"Mrs. Graham needed smelling salts," said Homer, "and didn't have any. So I gave her a drink of whisky. Choked her."

"How can you drink it!" cried Mrs. Graham. "I'll bet you could light a fire with it in the dead of winter."

"That's good whisky," said Homer, resentfully. "You should try and drink that nickel stuff—would take the hide off a buffalo and cure it. Now who in tarnation would be firing off a shotgun just for the fun of it?"

"Luis will find out," said Berta. "This is his territory, isn't it?"

"Yes," said Homer, "and welcome, I'm sure." But he was still resenting what Mrs. Graham had said about his own personal drinking-whisky, a pint of which he always carried about with him. "Went down the wrong way, Mrs. Graham," he said. "That's what it was."

"Homer," said Mrs. Graham, "there is no right way for that stuff. Now I know what the Indians mean by fire-water."

The discussion went on, Homer both resentful and plaintive, Mrs. Graham ironical. Berta was silent, thankful for the darkness. She was wildly, almost crazily happy. Staff would stay. She'd see him every day the rest of her life, she hoped. She was not too worried about the "trouble." She had great faith in Staff's ability to look after himself.

It was the first really cold night for weeks, and there was a rather sparse collection of loungers sprinkled along San Juan Street in front of Pop's corral and livery barn to watch Doc's triumphal progress from his house to the front door of the Palace.

Nine came, then nine fifteen. No Doc. Presently a few of the loungers started to drift away from their posts, some toward Howard Street, some inside the livery barn, where they could sit around the stove, which was lit for the first time that summer, put their feet up, and listen to the gossip about who had bought what horses and why.

Quiet settled down over San Juan Street. But at a little before nine-thirty, Doc appeared, wearing a dark overcoat and flanked by Pinto and Frenchy. Behind them, in pairs, straggled the Wardour brothers, then Leo Trotter and Pony Willis. With a stogie clamped tightly in the corner of his mouth, Doc looked unapproachable. There was no talking. The seven men just moved prosaically along toward another routine evening of fleecing the suckers at the Palace.

The loungers stared in silence. Doc was the big man now, the all-around big man of San Ygnacio, and growing with the town. These shiftless no-goods looked at him with awe, envying him, wondering how he did it.

As Doc and his retinue neared Howard, a tall man in a boat-shaped plains hat stepped out from the shadows thrown by the big corral posts at the far end of Pop's livery barn, and called across the street in a loud, clear voice:

"Doc—it's me, Brazos. Tell your boys not to make any funny movements. I've got men behind me in the corral with rifles."

Doc had stopped short. His men trod on each other's heels and cursed.

"Can you hear me, Doc?"

Doc leaned forward to peer across the street. "Yeah. I can hear you, Brazos. What do you want?"

Frenchy was cursing under his breath. "Got more lives than a cat, that dog of a dog!"

"You, tall fellow," Staff called to Pat Wardour, "watch your hands—or there'll be a massacre."

"Watch your hands, you goddamned fools," cried Doc, in an almost hysterically angry voice that unsettled his men badly.

"Doc, listen to me," called Staff, "you've run your string out. This town all of a sudden has got too small for

189

both of us. You should have listened to Ben Gann. He told you to get out. Now I'm telling you. You be on the Dayton Mills stage tomorrow morning. I'll be watching. If you're not—it's man to man right out in the middle of Howard Street. I don't trust you, Doc. So I am going to have a few fellows with rifles just in case. And if one of those fellows of yours makes a false move during the fight, he's a gone goslin'. Understand? And you're going to fight me whether you like it or not. You better show up. Or I'll come looking for you."

"Why, you stupid, cow-rassling horse-wrangler," shouted Doc, "you think I'd try to duck you? You be at Howard and San Juan as soon as that stage leaves. I'll be there."

"You better be, Doc," said Staff, "or your stock in this town will go down awful fast—you'll get chased out by fifteen-year-old Mexican boys."

Cursing violently, Doc turned on his heel and started for the Palace, followed by his retinue. Staff watched them till they had turned the corner, then he quickly climbed the corral fence and disappeared into the shadows.

There was blank consternation among the loungers who stood staring at each other in amazed horror. Then they began looking about for Mule Casper, who was a sort of leader in their set and would be able to tell them what to think; but this one night old Mule was missing. Finally they all began to talk excitedly. One man insisted that the tall fellow was "only that Stafford, who used to work for Pop." Another one cried: "It was Brazos! You heard him, didn't you? It was Brazos. Used to ride with the Kid. Can shoot the eyes out of a rattlesnake. That's what they say up north!"

The wrangling went on for a while, then stopped abruptly as Mule Casper came up puffing and limping. "This blasted cold weather started my rheumatism," cried Mule, "so I stayed in. What happened? What happened? I ran into Ez and he couldn't talk he was so excited."

Now Mule, listening in silence to various versions of the encounter, finally began to shake his head slowly. At last he said: "You can't beat them Mexicans. A man ought to listen to them closer. They said it was the Kid. And they weren't too far off. It was Brazos, Billy's pal and sidekick. Well, I never."

Pushing his way through the crowd, which was growing all the time now, he went inside the livery barn to find Pop. But Pop, sitting at his desk and looking a little pale and nervous as he puffed on his cigar, was already surrounded.

Mule pushed in rudely and confronted him. "Pop," he cried, "did you know that tall, lean fellow that was working for you was Brazos?"

Pop stubbornly shook his big head. "I wish you'd all shut up. You sound crazy. I don't know anything about it, only what I heard. Nothing at all. Nothing."

Finally the loungers scattered all over the town, to bars, to stores, to homes. In half an hour San Ygnacio was buzzing like a swarm of bees.

The five men rode in silence under the big moon: Staff, Ruy and Blasco Montez, Pete Lopez, and Pete's cousin from old Mexico, Pablo Diaz, who had just got in, couldn't speak a word of English, and grinned all the time. They were heavily armed with rifles, Colt revolvers, and shotguns.

It was a still night, without a suggestion of a breeze. Far across the tableland they could see the flickering naphtha flares of the labor camp at the spur.

Distant coyote voices punctuated the silence.

"See the big rock that looks like a church steeple?" asked Staff. "We'll camp there."

They rode into the black moon-shadow of the sixty-foot tall rock, dismounted and made camp.

"Pete," said Staff, "how about you take the first watch?"

"Okay," said Pete; then he laughed. "If they're hunting for you tonight in town, they'll get a big surprise."

Staff grinned. "And if they get real smart and figure I'll camp out for the night and come out this way, they'll get a bigger one."

Pablo chuckled in the darkness, although he didn't understand a word that had been said.

The dining-room at Ben Gann's house was full of milling people, and everybody was talking at once: Ben, the judge, Bob Gall, Luis, Homer, Joe Ballard, Juan Alvarez, and Al Tweedy. Berta, flushed and wildly excited, kept bringing in fresh coffee, helped by Homer, who was more than half tight.

In the confused babble of conversation, somebody was heard to remark that the thing had got so far along now that it would be impossible to stop it.

"Stop it?" shouted Ben Gann; then he tried to rise from his chair but fell back with a curse. "Who wants to stop it? Fair fight. Man to man. And we're going to see that it is."

"Ben, look," said Bob, "I'm just the marshal. I take care of drunks. I run out the riffraff, the scum. I can't step in and—"

"Homer," cried Ben, curtly breaking in on Bob's rather halfhearted protests, "you hear me? I want a horse and buggy from Pop Urbey's at the door at nine o'clock. I'm going to ride up to Howard and San Juan if I have to be lifted in. I'm taking a rifle along. And I'll shoot the first man that tries to interfere in this fight."

Homer cheered and waved his arms. Berta wanted to cheer also, but refrained.

"I admire your spirit, Ben," said Bob. "I sure do."

"He's a tough man, this fellow," cried Ben. "A brave man, tackling Doc. At least I was wearing a badge when I tangled with him."

There had been so much confusion and shouting ever since Luis had come with the news that Berta was almost certain that Ben did not know who "Brazos" really was. She moved over to him, leaned down and whispered:

"Do you know who he is?"

"Sure I know who he is," said Ben. "He's that tall fellow from the livery barn. Trying to live a decent life, I hear, and for some reason I don't understand, Doc wouldn't let him."

Berta burst into tears and ran from the dining-room into the kitchen. Ben looked after her, amazed.

"Call her back," he cried to Homer. "Call her back."

But she wouldn't come back.

Later, when they'd all gone, leaving Ben and Berta alone, Ben rattled his cane on the floor and shouted: "Berta, come in here. What's the matter with you?"

Berta came in with her eyes lowered and stood in front of her father.

"Now, what is all this?" he demanded. "Why were you crying like that?"

"It's Staff," said Berta. "I was happy."

"You were *what?*" cried Ben, staring.

"I was happy because of what you said."

Ben stared. "What did I say?"

"You said he was trying to lead a decent life and Doc wouldn't let him."

"All right," said Ben. "Why cry about that?"

"Because I'm going to marry him," said Berta.

Ben's cane slipped and he almost fell out of his chair. "You're going to do *what?* Are you crazy, Berta? What are you talking about?"

"I am going to marry Staff," said Berta, "and he's going to stay in San Ygnacio and work for Mr. Urbey."

Ben was grimly silent for a long time, and then he asked in an altered voice: "When did all this happen?"

"I saw him a few times," said Berta. "Once when I was riding out in the country he saved me from two horrible men. Ask Mrs. Graham. She was there. We talked, Staff and I. He told me about his life. He's been trying to live like other people."

"And you never told me anything about it," said Ben, looking at her reproachfully.

Berta lowered her eyes but said nothing.

In a moment Ben said thoughtfully: "Range-war fighter. Rode with Billy. So did a lot of pretty fair fellows."

There was a long silence and Ben sat staring at the floor. Finally he spoke. "We'll think about this, Berta. We'll talk it all over later. Now, ain't it way past your bedtime?"

Berta still said nothing, but impulsively leaned over Ben and gave him a smacking kiss on the cheek, then rushed from the room.

Ben sat sighing to himself. "He hit me right the only time I talked to him," he thought. "I hope he makes it against Doc. I sure hope he makes it."

Doc and his men had left the Palace early—two a.m.—and now Doc was pacing in the huge old living-room of his adobe house, with a stogie clamped in his mouth and his black Stetson down over his eyes. His men had argued with him till they were exhausted, and they were now lolling about limply.

There was a long silence. Finally Pinto couldn't stand it any longer and jumped up, startling Doc, who turned and gave him a wildly irritated glare. "But it's crazy, Doc. It's crazy. He's got no right. Let's hunt him down. He's got to be some place. How that crazy Barrows missed him with the two shotguns I gave him, I don't know."

"He's too smart for all of you," cried Doc. "He's a fox. You're all too stupid, so now I've got to settle him."

"But, Doc . . ." Pinto protested.

Now Doc whirled and stood glaring at them. "What's the matter? Lost your confidence in me? Think I can't take him—man to man? A lot of fellows have chosen me in twenty years, and where are they now? Buried, except for old Ben Gann, and he's as good as dead, creeping around like a crab, they tell me!" Now he screamed at them. "What the hell is the matter with all of you?"

They said nothing.

"Think I can't do it, eh?" cried Doc. "All right. Who wants to come out in the street with me right now—any two of you? I'll show you."

The men all shifted about uncomfortably and sat with lowered eyes. Doc wasn't making sense. He talked wild, crazy. They'd been riding high and living easy and they were badly spoiled. They cringed at the thought of losing all this. Why wouldn't Doc listen to reason?

"He challenged me publicly, didn't he?" cried Doc. "What kind of a yellow cur do you think I am?"

"But he had no right, Doc, no right," whined Pinto.

"No right, eh?" said Doc, laughing sardonically. "Oh, no. No right at all. We've tried to kill him three times. No, he's got no right at all."

"He can't prove nothing," said Pat Wardour.

"What is this, a court of law?" cried Doc. "What does he have to prove? He just challenged me in public, so I've got to get out or fight. You want me to get out?"

"Doc, Doc," Pinto protested.

"You want me to get a bellyache and send one of you instead? How about you, Pat? Will you go?"

Pat squirmed and made no answer. What could he say? Doc wouldn't let him take his place, anyway. It was all just so much wind and chin-music. "I sure am surprised at Doc," he thought, moving uncomfortably and keeping his eyes lowered.

"All of you go to bed. Get out," shouted Doc. "I'm sick of the sight of you."

* * *

In his own room now, with the door closed and the faint noises of the town coming in through an open window, Doc sat down to write a letter.

Dear Kate:

Charley sent me your last address and I hope this reaches you. Charley tells me you are doing all right in Dallas and I'm sure glad. I think about you quite a lot and I'm damned sorry I treated you the way I did. Stay away from the dives; keep working like you are. Restaurant business is a good business. Not so many cheap tin-horns and bums.

Well, Kate, I guess you will be surprised to hear from me. The last time we talked you called me a low son of a bitch and wished I'd drop dead. But we all say things like that when we're mad. I've said more or less the same to you. I didn't mean it. And maybe you didn't.

The years pass and I get older—I was forty-one yesterday—and I frankly don't know what it's all about, Kate. I hope you do.

This letter may sound crazy to you, but tomorrow's a big day for me, a real big day, and that's why I'm writing, as I can't talk to you. Kate, let me say this, you are the only woman in this world I ever really cared a damn about, and why I acted the way I did with you, I don't know.

If anything should happen to me, Ross Bagley will send you on quite a hunk of money. I'll take care of it first thing in the morning. Buy yourself your own restaurant.

Well, goodnight. It's three-thirty a.m. and I've got to get some sleep. Goodnight, Kate.

As ever,
Doc

By nine o'clock the next morning, Howard Street was swarming with men. At nine fifteen, to everybody's astonishment, Ben Gann appeared in a buggy driven by

Homer Smith. Men called greetings to him and even waved their hats; it was like old times, seeing the marshal again. But why did the buggy stop a few feet down from the front of the Long Horn Hotel and stay there?

Time passed. Now there was great activity in the stage station as the Dayton Mills stage began to make up. The six horses were led into the shafts and harnessed; the shotgun messenger stood on the porch, smoking his pipe and showing off his guns, proud of the heavy artillery; the Wells Fargo box was thrown up, also the mail sacks. Little by little, the passengers began to take their places. The stage was going to be loaded, overloaded, if anything—with half-a-dozen men, aside from the messenger, riding on the top.

Old Mule came limping out of the station and hurried over to a crowd of loungers on the northeast corner of Howard and San Juan. "Doc's staying," he said. "Didn't buy no ticket."

Somebody guffawed. "You call that news? Of course he's staying. He'll shoot the daylights out of that crazy cowhand from the livery barn."

"Even money says he don't," said somebody else. "That there's Brazos, that cowhand. A dead shot."

"Looks like a skinny boy to me."

"That's because you're so dadblamed old yourself."

More guffaws.

"Stage is about ready," called Mule, and a wave of excitement passed over the crowd. "Yep. She's ready now. She'll be off in a minute. He's picking up the reins. . . ."

Across the street, the stage-driver kicked off the brake, gave the reins a jerk and hollered like an Apache Indian ready for the kill. The old stage creaked and groaned and lurched in its straps, and at last gave a convulsive start, the men on the top swaying wildly and grabbing at anything for support.

"Yo! Yo! Yo! Yo!" screamed the driver, cracking his long whip over the horses' backs, and the Dayton Mills stage was on its way, raising a huge cloud of dust that billowed slowly upward and then hung in a long, horizontal bar over the street before it settled.

"There she goes," cried Mule, "and it oughtn't to be long now before the ball is opened. Sashay all!" Mule held up his coat-tails and cut a caper or two.

The loungers laughed nervously. That Mule! He'd dance and sing at his own funeral.

Suddenly one of the loungers grabbed Mule and pointed. "Look way up the street. See?" He was shaking with excitement.

"Yeah, yeah," said Mule. "That's Brazos, all right."

Staff was walking straight down the middle of Howard Street, limping slightly. He'd just turned in from the Mexican settlement. His boat-shaped hat was on the back of his head and he looked no different than he looked at the livery barn, except for the guns: blue flannel shirt, tight jean pants out over worn boots.

"Look behind him," called Mule.

Four men with rifles were following him, deployed across the street. As Staff came on, they dropped farther and farther behind, and finally took up posts that commanded the whole corner of San Juan and Howard.

"Taking no chances, that fellow," said one of the loungers.

"Yes, sir," said Mule. "It's going to be man to man, or he'll know the reason why. He just don't trust them boys of Doc's."

Luis sat watching Berta narrowly. Ben had warned him not to let her out of his sight. But she showed no signs whatever of any nervousness or disturbance, but sat darning one of her father's socks. And Luis could not help thinking: "Imagine having a girl like that darning your socks!" To Luis, it seemed slightly sacrilegious.

But he did notice that from time to time she glanced up at the clock, and then seemed to be listening.

As for himself, Luis was so nervous and overwrought that he could hardly sit still.

"Is that clock right, Luis?" Berta asked finally.

"Yes," said Luis.

"The stage has pulled out then," said Berta.

"Might have got delayed," said Luis. "Sometimes Burke is behindhand with the mail sacks."

After a long silence, Berta said: "I wish it was over. But he'll win, Luis; you'll see; he'll win."

"Of course he will, Miss Berta," said Luis, but actually, Luis was in despair. He felt a terrible awe of the slit-eyed little doctor. Top gun of the West. Wasn't that what they called him?

Staff was nearing the corner now, walking very slowly, his big hands hanging loosely near his guns. But Doc was nowhere to be seen. Men kept craning their necks and questioning the people about them. The stage had disappeared into the distance long ago. Where was Doc?

Finally he appeared from the front door of the Palace. He was dressed as he had been the day that he arrived in San Ygnacio, except for the coat. Pink shirt, with a white collar and black string tie; tight black pants out over his boots; and a black Stetson. There was a stogie clamped in the side of his mouth. Behind him came Pinto and Frenchy, then the Wardours, then, finally, Pony Willis and Leo Trotter, who did not seem any too anxious to come out into the blazing sunlight of Howard Street.

Ben leaned down in the buggy and shouted across at Doc. "I'm watching your boys, Doc." Then he brandished the rifle.

Doc seemed painfully surprised at Ben's presence. "You don't give up easy, do you, Ben?" called Doc.

"No," said Ben. "I'll outlive you yet."

Doc tried to laugh, but it didn't seem to come out right, sounding more like a cough. He pulled the stogie out of his mouth, looked at it angrily, then threw it away.

His boys fanned out along the sidewalk in front of the Palace, Pinto and Frenchy at the most exposed place near the corner, Pony Willis and Leo Trotter as far away as they could get without seeming to hide. The Wardours were in the middle and they both stood picking their teeth nervously.

Now Doc stepped down from the curb, tilted his hat over his eyes and looked off to the north. Staff was standing in the middle of the street in front of the stage station, relaxed, waiting.

Little by little, the street cleared, as men drew back into doorways and alleyways out of the line of fire.

Doc seemed to hesitate, and stood pulling at his under lip.

"All right, Doc," called Staff. "I'm coming. Start shooting whenever you're ready."

Doc planted his feet apart and waited. He was gripped by a feeling of despair. Ever since Staff had called to him from across the street the night before, he had felt that this was the big last one that he couldn't win. Even old Ben Gann had knocked him down. Forty-one, a ripe age for the frontier. A very ripe age. Hickok had always contended that a man's reflexes started to go after he was twenty-six years old. Doc laughed sadly and sardonically to himself.

Staff kept coming, slowly and relentlessly, his eyes narrowed, his lips grim.

A nervous silence fell like a dark cloud over Howard Street.

Ben gritted his teeth and shrank a little in his clothes. They were both waiting too long. Far too long. Those guns they were wearing were almost as accurate as rifles at a fairly good range. It was all draw now; all draw!

Suddenly Doc reached, but before his gun-barrel was tilted upward, Staff had drawn and fired twice. A look of amazement showed in Doc's grim face, he staggered forward a step or two, dropped his gun, stumbled, then fell face down in the thick dust of Howard Street, raising a small cloud, which hung motionless above him for a moment.

Nobody spoke. Everybody was stunned by the swift conclusion. There was utter silence. Men stood frozen in various attitudes, staring blankly.

But then suddenly Pinto went berserk. Sobbing like a child, he ran out into the middle of the street, bent down to Doc, and rolled him over. Doc's eyelids fluttered slightly. "Kate," he said. "She'll get it now . . . the restaurant . . ."

"What, Doc? What?" sobbed Pinto.

Doc's head rolled away from Pinto. His eyes closed. Yelling like a maniac, Pinto jumped to his feet. It was obvious that he was going for his guns.

Staff screamed at him: "Don't do it, pink eye. Don't do it."

The shrill voice seemed to penetrate. Pinto hesitated; his hands stopped halfway. Now Frenchy rushed out into the street, grabbed Pinto and pulled him into the Palace. They were followed slowly by the Wardours, and quickly by Leo Trotter and Pony Willis.

Dr. Ortega crossed the empty street now and bent down to examine Doc's body, remembering, as he did so, what Doc had said the night he'd disemboweled the drunken Texan in the gambling room: "The operation was successful, but the patient died."

About the Author

The late W. R. Burnett was born in Springfield, Ohio. He was educated at schools in Columbus and Germantown, and attended Ohio State University for two years. He started writing in earnest while doing statistical work for the Ohio Bureau of Workmen's Compensation. His first big success, LITTLE CAESAR, was published in 1929. In all, he wrote more than twenty novels, including IRON MAN; DARK HAZARD; HIGH SIERRA; and more recently, THE ASPHALT JUNGLE; LITTLE MEN, BIG WORLD; VANITY ROW; ADOBE WALLS; and PALE MOON; many short stories, which appeared in such magazines as *Collier's*, *Harper's*, and the *Saturday Evening Post*, and were included in the O. Henry and O'Brien collections of best short stories; and a number of screenplays.